Praise for *The Neversink Chronicles*

Books by John Dwaine McKenna:

The Neversink Chronicles

The Whim-Wham Man

Coming in early 2013:

The Colorado Noir Chronicles

The Whim-Wham Man

By
John Dwaine McKenna

RHYOLITE PRESS, LLC

Published in the United States of America by Rhyolite Press, LLC
P.O. Box 2406
Colorado Springs, Colorado 80901
www.rhyolitepress.com

McKenna, John Dwaine
The Whim-Wham Man / John Dwaine McKenna
1st ed. August 2012

Library of Congress Control Number: 2012914922
ISBN 978-0-9839952-1-0
(eBook ISBN 978-0-9839952-4-1)

PRINTED IN THE UNITED STATES OF AMERICA
1st edition
Cover design and book design by Donald R. Kallaus
Author photo, © Donald R. Kallaus, 2012

Cover art: *Mountain Landscape, 1878* George Caleb Bingham
© Starsmore Center for Local History
Colorado Springs, Colorado

This is for all the children
the innocent ones
the victims

One

The Whim-Wham man's story ain't easy to tell.

It happened in the spring of 1940. I was fifteen years old, and big for my age. You might even say I was man-sized; I know my Pa worked me like one. But that's the way it was back then, when the family was living up in Husted, twelve miles or so north of Colorado Springs. Husted was where the Air Force Academy is now. Our one-hundred-acre place was about where the football stadium sits today, and we were hanging on to it by the skin of our teeth and the Grace of God. The bad times were in the tenth year, and folks were just about wore out. Sure, there were great times in the twenties: prices were high, the stock was fat, glossy and sleek from clover and alfalfa all summer, and life was good, the living easy. Ma said it's when Pa started in drinking heavy and abusing her. But then came the crash in twenty-nine, followed a couple of years later by the drought, and the dust . . . and the Great Depression. Ma told me that Pa had mortgaged the place, to get us through a personal bad year that turned into two bad years, that turned into ten-eleven-twelve years, about as fast as you can snap your fingers.

So, like I said, we were staying a half-step ahead of the bank. Pa caught a break in thirty-nine and landed a temporary job with the Denver & Rio Grande Railroad, as a maintenance man over at the roundhouse in Husted. It turned into a more or less permanent position, although with those big new diesels coming on, it was anybody's guess how long the steam locomotives he worked on would last. Ma brought in a little cash by selling eggs, butter and hand-picked wild berries to the Hardy House up in Palmer Lake. She'd take my two little sisters, Annie and Catherine, and the three of them would pick wild strawberries, raspberries, blueberries . . . whatever was in season . . . clean, wash and cull the bad ones for ten cents a quart. Delivered. And those wild berries are less than half the size of store-bought ones. It was a lot of work, but we were damn glad for the cash money. I took care of our stock, and hired out for wages whenever one of the other ranchers needed an extra hand: haying, calving or butchering time mostly. Every so often, I'd take my horse and a mule up in the foothills and bring back a deer, once or twice an elk, even an antelope now and again. We'd eat good for a while, and Ma would have an extra bit of cash from the meat she sold to Tony, the cook at the Hardy House. He charged premium prices for venison and elk steaks from the train riders. Fact is, I've left many a hindquarter at the back door of the place in the gray light just before the sun comes up. Tony or his helper, an old broken-down cowboy name of Petey, always had a hot cup of coffee for me. Sometimes a piece of pie. And more often than not, the buckskin quarter horse I called Duffy, got a carrot or two. We helped each other, so we'd all make it through the Depression. It's just the way it was.

Two

The first time we saw the Whim-Wham man, Ma and I, along with little Annie and Catherine, were going to Colorado Springs. Ma had extra butter and egg money she was going to invest in some cloth for dresses for her and the girls, maybe even a couple of shirts for Pa and me. Ma had thinned out her hens and four or five roosters. Tony had specials going on roast chicken, while Ma was all set for some new clothes. I was going to Templeton's, the grainery down at the railyards on Sierra Madre Street, for a few sacks of horse and chicken feed, a salt lick for the cattle and a few other farm and ranch supplies we needed.

We were headed for town in our truck, an old T-Model Ford, the kind with three transmission pedals and a hand throttle, when Annie, sitting in Ma's lap said, "Look, Mama."

"Where, child?"

"Over there. At the funny man."

We were just crossing the wooden trestle bridge over Monument Creek, down past the Brickman place. Annie was pointing to a copse of cottonwoods growing alongside the stream where it ran close to the road. It was a spot where we'd had campers before. The train tracks made an S curve to cross the creek and wind around a pair of small mesas. The engineers had to slow the trains down, and it was a perfect spot for the traveling men—the bums and hobos—to hop on and off. They'd gather in a camp down there called a jungle, until the sheriff and his deputies came once or twice each summer and fall to roust them out and move them along. Each spring when the weather got warm, the jungle would set up again, as the bums began to come back and the whole thing would be reborn. With the Depression and all, a lot of them were just guys trying to find work. It was hard not to feel sorry for them, but like Pa said, we had to look out for our own.

Smoke from the campfire was rising up through the young mint-colored leaves where a hobo was sitting on a rock, heating a can of something or other. He nodded politely as I motored on by at a stately twenty-five miles per hour, and the girls both waved to him. Catherine said, "Who was that, Mama?"

"A traveling man."

"What's that?"

"A traveling man goes from place to place, always moving about."

"Doesn't he have a home?"

"No. He doesn't."

"Oh. That's sad. But he still looks funny."

"There'll be no more of that kind of talk, girls."

I noticed a red-and-black flannel shirt he was wearing, as well as an old beat-up brown fedora and a piece of rope for a belt. He had frizzy hair like a negro and a straggly beard, but it was his reddish brown skin, the color of mahogany wood, that was his most arresting feature. I'd never seen anything like it. I looked over and said, "He does look different, Ma."

She nodded. "He looks to be of mixed blood: negro, white and Indian—probably Cherokee. I saw a few others like him when your father and I got married, when we took the train to New Orleans for our wedding trip. I think the people down there called them red-bones, like the hound. It isn't a flattering thing to say, James."

"Yes, Ma," was all I could think of to say. The musical lilt of her brogue reminded me again of her childhood in Dublin. She'd grown up in a mansion of the upper classes . . . where her mother was a housemaid. When the lord of the manor began making lewd advances at her, and her own mother said, "You'll get used to it," she stole money from the house cash account and fled to the United States. She'd come down the ship's gangway and almost fell into the arms of a young marine just back from the Great War in the spring of 1919. His name was Frank McGoran. My father and his bride, Eileen O'Shaunaghessy, have been together ever since.

Three

Cars and a couple of small trucks passed us as I puttered along on Nevada Avenue toward downtown. Even though we were holding up traffic, I held it at twenty-five miles per hour. Any faster, and I was afraid of blowing a tire. There wasn't any spare, nor money for one.

"You know," Ma said, breaking into my thoughts, "he looked like a whim-wham man to me. I haven't seen one since I left home"

By "home" I knew she meant Ireland, not Husted. As if she could read my mind, she added, "A whim-wham man sells trinkets and notions. Small things he can carry on his back or make by hand from things he finds as he walks about. We'll see on the way back. He'll have things laid out for sale."

I turned right, onto Pikes Peak Avenue, then south on Tejon Street, dropped Ma and the girls off at Hibbards Department Store.

"I'll park out here when I get done at Templeton's. Figure an hour and a half or so, time I get loaded."

Ma waved, the girls were making a beeline for the front door. I let up on the brake, opened the throttle a notch and turned west on Colorado

Avenue, heading for the grainery on Sierra Madre Street.

I parked and went in, gave them the money Ma and I'd scraped up and our order, written in pencil on a brown paper sack. I was sitting on some hundred-pound burlap bags of corn, reading a Gazette-Telegraph someone had left when I heard a voice . . .

"Hey boy, what're ya doing, sitting on my feed?"

I stood, put the paper down and prepared to apologize, before I saw the speaker.

"Hello, Mister Brickman."

He was our neighbor to the south, a man I'd hired out to any number of times. He was a good neighbor and a fair man to work for, even though you'd be plumb wore out and ready to turn in after working for him all day. He was also the father of Rueben, my oldest friend, and Madeline-Jean, my sister Catherine's "very best friend." Rueben was a few years older than me and was like the big brother I'd never had.

"How's the folks, Jamey?"

"They're okay. How's Rueben?"

"Good. He's still up in Boulder, going to summer school so he can graduate sooner."

"Tell him hello."

"I will. I've got some work next week if you're able."

"What day?"

"Come Monday at breakfast."

"I'll be there. Ma's gonna ask about Missus Brickman and Maddie."

"Sadie's good, feeding me like a hog. I'm sure Maddie would love to see Catherine if you want to bring her."

Before I had a chance to answer, Old Man Templeton himself came from the office. Nodding to Mr. Brickman, he looked at me.

"James McGoran. I appreciate your Pa paying his account down some. But with these new supplies, the bill's still growing. You tell Frank I'd like to see him. Okay? Your order's out on the dock. But I can't keep on doing this. You tell Frank to come see me."

"See you Monday," I said to Mr. Brickman and headed for the door, head down, cheeks flaming in embarrassment.

"Bring Catherine," was the last thing I heard as I went outside.

Four

I crossed Sierra Madre Street heading for our Model T, passing Mr. Brickman's new truck on my way. It was a one-and-a-half-ton Ford, the COE, or cab-over-engine model, with a V-eight engine and a PTO hoist which raised the bed . . . like a dump truck. It was slick as a cat's whiskers and really nice at haying season, when all you had to do to unload her was pull down the lever and let the clutch out. Red in color, with snap-ring wheels, she was a honeydripper for sure. I passed close enough to run my hand up, over and down her fender. Damn. She was pretty.

Guess Mister Brickman has all the luck, I thought. Coal had been discovered under a big part of his property. He'd sold the sub-surface mining rights to the True-West Coal Company back in the twenties, Ma said. *He's rich, but even so, he gets all its worth out of every dollar.*

When I got to our truck, I climbed in, set the spark and throttle, pulled the choke out a teeny bit, made sure the hand-brake was all the way back and pulled the crank out from under the driver's seat.

I walked around front, stuck the crank in the hole at the base of the radiator. I made sure it was seated properly and worked it around to the seven o'clock position. Then, I gave it a hard yank. The old Model T started right up.

Like Pa said, "She's a homely old girl, but reliable."

Ma always said, "You shush, Frank." When she did, he'd grin like he'd said something funny. *Beats me*, I thought at the time.

I jumped up in the driver's seat and retarded the spark a little, put my left foot on the left pedal, pushed halfway down, then shoved the center pedal in all the way and let it out, backed across the street, squared up to the loading dock, idled the motor down and reset the brake. Only then did I get out and jump up on the dock as a couple of Templeton's men came out pushing a four-wheeled cart with our small bunch of animal feed and ranch supplies on it. We transferred it all, and I went up the street to get Ma and the girls. As I did, I decided that driving a Model T was not for sissies.

Ma and the girls were standing on the sidewalk. They held bundles wrapped in brown paper and tied with string, waiting as I pulled up.

"Would you ladies like a ride?"

"Can I ride in the back with Catherine?"

"You can if your sister will hold on to you, and you both stay seated."

"I will, Mama."

"Catherine?"

"Yes, Mama. I'll hold her."

I jumped up in the bed and rearranged feed sacks until there was space for them. The girls nestled down where Ma could see them through the back window. They settled while Ma watched, and I climbed back in the cab, checked the street, but we were the only vehicle. I pulled out and headed north, in the direction of Husted, and home.

I held the old truck under twenty miles an hour, worried about blowing a back tire with the added weight. Ma was keeping an eye on the girls and chatting up a storm, but I wasn't really hearing her, thinking about what Old Man Templeton had said. *Whatever would we do without grain, or salt, or the million other things we needed to run a ranch . . .*

Ma pulled my sleeve.

"Jamey. What's the matter?"

"Nothing. Just thinking is all."

"Sure, and you look like you're carrying the weight of the world on your shoulders. What happened over there?"

"At Templeton's?"

She didn't say anything when I glanced at her, but she stared at me with her left eyebrow lifted in an arch, her way of expressing exasperation. The way she did it made her face look like a caterpillar was inching along on her brow, and gave her a kind of scowl. It made her face look odd, and unnatural.

"So?" she said, letting go of my sleeve and relaxing her face. She gave a quick look back at Annie and Catherine, sitting together between hundred-pound burlap sacks.

"They're okay, Ma. I'm watching them in the mirrors and we ain't moving fast enough to do much hurt."

"Don't say ain't. It makes you sound like a bog-Irish peat digger."

"Aren't. We are not going fast enough." And I told her what Otis Templeton had said in front of Mr. Brickman.

"He said that in front of Morrie . . . Mister Brickman?"

"Yes, Ma. He did."

"The old buzzard himself. Said that."

"Yes, Ma."

13

Even at the snail's pace I was driving, we were almost to the wooden bridge over Monument Creek by the time I'd finished telling her about it. We were on the edge of the Brickman place . . . where the Whim-Wham man had set up shop while we were downtown. When I drove over the bridge, we could see smoke from his campfire again, and a canvas covered shelter he'd rigged up like a lean-to. On the side closest to the road he'd spread another piece of canvas with trinkets he'd made by whittling pieces of driftwood. He was sitting on a rock he'd rolled up from the creek, strumming a battered old guitar with the end of a wooden drumstick.

I could tell she was angry and upset by the line of her jaw and the flush on her face. Ma had dark hair back then, bright blue eyes and a fair complexion that flushed when she got upset, and burned bright red when embarrassed; most usually by something Pa would whisper in her ear. She was still thinking about what I'd told her as I crossed the bridge and the campsite appeared.

"Stop, Jamey, I want to see what he has."

I pulled over, shut the motor off with the magneto switch, got out and lifted Annie down to the ground. She ran after Ma and Catherine, eager to see what the funny-looking man was doing. I got the canvas water bag we carried behind the seat, figuring I'd take the opportunity to walk over to the creek and get water to add to the radiator. The truck was steaming some from pulling the grade up out of Colorado Springs, loaded down with feed. I'd have to walk right by the camp, and to tell the truth, I wanted to see what he was doing myself.

The smell hit me like a fist in the face during a schoolyard scrap before I was halfway across the road. It was plain to me that the Whim-Wham man was a stranger to soap and water: he smelled as bad as a dog who'd been rolling in a ten day old carcass. Annie and Catherine

14

were in retreat, headed back to the safety of their perch up on the truck. Ma had a handkerchief to her face as she looked over the items he was offering. The Whim-Wham man himself was sitting on the same rock, but now he was strumming his out-of-tune guitar with half of a wooden drumstick—even though the third string from the bottom was missing—like a child who doesn't know any better. He continued without any sense or purpose I could tell, all the while watching Annie and Catherine as they went back aboard the truck. I stepped into his line of sight and stopped.

"Ma, will you be okay long enough for me to go over to the creek and get water?"

She looked at me and nodded. The Whim-Wham man was speeding up his tempo on the guitar until he was beating so hard the drumstick was a blur and the sounds it made were almost unbearable to hear. And then he stopped. He sighed and put the guitar down, looked up at me and smiled. It was then I saw he had the face of a moron, or an imbecile. He was an unfortunate, an idiot, whose lopsided grin was allowing a stream of drool to leak out. Why he wasn't in an insane asylum, I'll never know. I looked at him and pointed to his chin, wiped my mouth with my sleeve. He did the same, the crooked grin never leaving his face, his brown eyes never leaving mine. They were the saddest ones I'd ever seen, vacant as the dust-blown prairies east of here, where only the most desolate kind of life lived. His eyes were like brown pools that had no source. Sad eyes, they held only resignation, of a life at the very bottom . . . a life without friends, home or family . . . a life with no sort of society, and no hope of comfort.

Five

I filled the water bag at the creek and walked back to see how Ma was doing.

"Jamey, come here and look at these carvings. They're remarkable."

I went over to where she was sitting on a piece of canvas with her knees bent and legs tucked under her skirt. There was an assortment of carvings in her lap: birds, fish, rabbits, snakes, frogs, turtles, deer, bears, alligators, possums, dogs, cats, owls, foxes and squirrels were carved in intricate detail from pieces of wood. No two were alike and all were animated . . . so lifelike . . . I expected them to jump, slither, swim or fly away.

Ma looked at the man, sitting on a rock across the campfire with his battered guitar lying on the cheatgrass beside him. She pointed to the carvings at her side, "How much?"

"I don't know."

"Are they for sale?"

"I dunno."

Ma picked out a dozen different ones, put them in a group in front of her.

"I dunno," the Whim-Wham man said in his high voice.

"Ma, I don't think he knows what you mean. Try offering him some money. Have you got some coins? Try those."

Ma took her change purse out, extracted a handful of pennies, nickels and dimes, put them on the canvas, in front of the carvings. She pushed the pile toward the Whim-Wham man and pulled the carvings toward her.

He looked at the coins and shook his head.

"What now, Jamey?"

"Maybe he wants more."

Ma went back to her change purse, extracted a quarter and put it in the pile. "That's it. Sure, and it's a whole lot of berry picking at ten cents the quart."

He looked at Ma for a long moment then looked at the pile of change and nodded to Ma. As she was gathering her treasure, the man stood and went to his lean-to. When he came back, he handed me a carving and handed something to Ma, pointed to the truck.

"What's he giving you?"

"A pair of carved dolls for the girls. You?"

"It's a coyote, howling at the moon."

It looked so real, I almost thought I could hear his song. I looked at the Whim-Wham man and said, "Thank you," but he didn't seem to hear . . . he was too busy picking coins up, one by one, and grinning like the Cheshire Cat.

Six

The girls were happy to have the dolls, especially Annie, who was soon playing with hers. Catherine was older, and out of the dolly phase, but she was a good sport about it, and they both stood in the truck bed waving their thank-yous to the Whim-Wham man, who waved back at them and watched as I drove up the road.

As it turned out, I didn't have to tell Pa what Otis Templeton said, because Ma did, as we ate supper that night when he got home from the roundhouse. Then, after Annie was put to bed, while Catherine washed and I dried the dishes, Ma and Pa went for a long walk. It was well past dark when they came back. Catherine had gone to bed, and I was ready myself, having concluded the chapter of the book I was reading. Ma looked grim, and I could tell that she'd been crying. Pa was a thundercloud about to explode when they came up the porch steps and into the parlor together, still holding hands. I flinched when Pa put his hand on my shoulder as he passed by but said nothing.

I smelled the liquor on him, and hoped he didn't have enough booze around the place to get juiced up good and proper. Ma kissed me on the cheek and they went in their room and closed the door. I turned out the lights and went to my own bedroom for the night, hoping for the best.

Monday morning I was up before dawn. I went out and checked the stock, caught Duffy and saddled up, left him tied to the porch railing. It'd been a long, odd weekend. Ma and Pa were short with each other and the atmosphere was tense. Pa kept working on a bottle he had hid somewhere, and all of us were walking on eggshells. Even little Annie was quiet. It could have been because she was coming down with a cold . . . she started sniffling and running a temperature Sunday morning, and by afternoon Ma had put her in bed. Ma said it was a kid thing, but I wondered if it was from riding home in the back of the truck.

I spread some corn for the chickens, even though they were still roosting, figuring it would save Ma a little work. When I went in the house to fill a couple of canteens, Catherine was waiting for me.

"Well good morning. What are you doing up so early?"

"I'm going with you, to see Maddie."

"Oh. I forgot," I said with a smile. It was all she'd talked about on Sunday. "Are you ready to go? Did you leave a note for Ma?"

"No. She's in with Annie."

I finished filling the canteens at the pump by the kitchen sink. I took extra water because there was no telling what Mr. Brickman would have me doing, or where I'd be all day. I sliced off some bread and cheese, checked the icebox for meat but didn't find any. I wrapped it all in a dish towel and put it in my saddlebags, along with my rain slicker. Ma came in with a basin and dumped it in the sink. She still had her housecoat on and her hair was down.

"How's she doing?"

"Sleeping. She's got a fever, but she'll be okay. It's just the sniffles. Kid stuff. Do you have lunch, just in case?"

"Bread and cheese. No meat. "

"We ate it all last night. There's venison jerky in the pantry."

I went in, grabbed a handful and put it in my saddlebags with the other stuff and tossed it over my shoulder.

"Let's go, Catherine."

I kissed Ma on the cheek and went out to where Duffy waited, with Catherine right behind me.

"Say hello to Sadie for me."

"Yes, Ma. I will."

I climbed aboard Duffy and pulled Catherine up behind. We headed for the Brickmans in the gray light some call the false dawn that comes before the first sign of the sun. As the light came over the eastern plains, it looked like it was going to be a pretty day. But looks are often deceiving; what started with such promise in the false light of dawn grew into the worst day of my life before it was over.

Duffy was feeling good, snorting and biting at the bit. My arms were wearing out reining him in.

"He's sure full of vinegar."

"He wants to run."

"Yeah, but Ma would never forgive me if I let you fall off and get hurt."

"I won't. Let him go, Jamey."

Catherine, like me, had learned to ride before she learned to walk and was at home on horseback.

"You got a good hold of me?"

"Yeah. Do it."

I eased up on the reins and the horse stepped off at a fast trot that became an easy canter. We ate up the miles and pulled into the Brickmans front yard just as the sun busted the horizon in a dazzle of orange, pinks and reds that filled the whole sky . . . and reminded me of what a tiny speck I was in such a large uncaring universe.

Seven

I let Catherine down at the front door.

"I'm going to walk Duffy, cool him down. Tell Missus Brickman, I'll be right there."

Catherine nodded, and went up the steps to the porch to knock on the front door. It opened almost as soon as her fingers reached for the iron bell mounted to the middle of it.

Looks like Maddie's as excited as Catherine, I thought as I walked Duffy down to the main barn to find some feed sacks to wipe the sweat off of him. I left him saddled, and walked him back to the house. Mr. Brickman was sitting on the porch railing with a cup of coffee in his hand, watching me.

"I swear Jamey, you treat that horse better'n I treated my first girlfriend."

"You were only twelve years old," Mrs. Brickman said from the open doorway behind him. "And besides which, I threw you over for that cute George Douthit."

"Yeah. But I won your heart."

"Well c'mon handsome. Your breakfast awaits."

I tied Duffy up, took off my old cowboy hat and followed them in.

Mrs. Brickman had a huge meal spread out: platters of fried eggs, ham and a big bowl of home-fried potatoes with onions, and a basketful of hot biscuits that were complemented by milk and coffee. She also had strawberry jam that was as good as Ma's, and I ate like a wolf. A starving wolf.

Mr. Brickman pushed his mustache away from his face with his right thumb and blew on his coffee, took a sip. He put the mug down and said, "Dang, son, I'd hate to feed you when you was hungry."

"Oh stoppit, Morrie," his wife said. "It's good to see him eat. Would you like another biscuit, Jamey?"

"Thanks. They're really good."

I'd practically grown up in this house . . . the Brickmans were like my own relatives, and I was used to Mr. Brickman's joshing. And I knew he wasn't serious when he said something like that. I put jam and a piece of ham on the biscuit, polished it off in three bites.

"Thank you Missus Brickman for the nice breakfast. It was real good. And Ma said to tell you hello."

"You're welcome. How is your mother?"

"She's fine. Working hard like always. She just got done thinning out her hens and a couple of roosters."

"Figured she did. I saw in the paper where the Hardy House has had roasted chicken all week."

I grinned, "It was a massacre for a while. Blood, feathers and squawking all over the place. The survivors are laying eggs like mad."

"I bet they are. They know somehow."

"Pa says it's the chicken party line."

"Mr. Brickman drained his mug. "How is your pa?"

He said it in his quiet voice, but it was a loaded question. Everybody knew Pa had taken to drinking more than he should've. Maybe because of the worry over paying the bills . . . or maybe because of the things he saw "over there," during the Great War. Then again, maybe he just had a natural built-in inclination for it. I've noticed since then, that some men do. But back on that day in 1940, I was still just fifteen years old, no matter how grown-up I looked. A man looking for a reason to drink can always find one. My pa had his and everybody knew it. My answer was slow, and careful, and deliberate. "He's still working for the D&RG, up at the roundhouse."

Mr. Brickman was careful with his answer too. "Good. Real good. He must be doing a good job for them."

I didn't have any answer, just shrugged and took a last sip of coffee. Pa hadn't quit drinking, not by a long shot.

Eight

Mr. Brickman put his napkin next to his plate and looked at his wife.

"I hope I can get enough work outta this boy to pay for all the grub he's packing in."

Mrs. Brickman stood up and began clearing the dishes. She patted me on the shoulder and said, "Don't you listen to a word he says, Jamey. You eat all you want. I'm going to make you a nice big lunch too."

"Now I know I'm not gonna make any money today."

Mr. Brickman shook his head in mock sorrow. He was smiling and his eyes were all crinkled up at the corners. He looked at me, "You ready to go to work then?"

"Yes sir."

I took a last drink of milk and stood.

"Thanks again for the wonderful breakfast Missus Brickman. It was great."

She reached up and hugged my shoulder.

"You're welcome. Glad to see you eat like that."

Mr. Brickman leaned down and kissed her on the lips.

"We'll be down at number five, clearing it out. It'll take most of the day."

He put a beat-up old brown fedora with a small brim on his head.

"Where's the girls?"

"Up in Maddie's room. They got biscuits and jam first thing. They're up there sharing secrets. I think they're going on a picnic later down by the creek."

"Tell them to be careful by the water, there's snakes."

I spoke up, "I seen a couple of campfires in the jungle when I rode in this morning."

"The bums've been thick down there all spring. Lots of traveling men, with the depression and all. Sadie, tell the girls to stay away from the creek. Too many strange people around."

I put my hat on and followed Mr. Brickman into the morning sunlight. The clock on the kitchen wall showed it was almost seven.

"We're going to clear out house number five, so you won't need your pony. You can put him in the corral or the pasture, whichever you want."

I unsaddled Duffy and led him down to the pasture, where I took his bridle off and turned him out. He snorted, then moved off a little ways in the knee-deep grass and started grazing.

"He's a good-looking animal."

"Smart too. He comes when I whistle."

Nine

For the next five hours I was up to my elbows in dust, feathers and hard-packed chicken shit. Clearing house number five was a simple, hard-work job. The chickens had been sold to a processing plant in Denver. They came down and took all five thousand of the resident birds, so cleaning the chicken house was easy, but hard, like I said. Every couple of years the manure, dust and cast-off feathers had built up a layer about four inches thick. My job was to chip and scrape it off the floor with a straight-bladed hoe, then shovel it out an open window into a manure spreader. A manure spreader is a box-like wagon pulled by a horse or a tractor. It has gears that turn big propellers at the back of it that chop the manure up and fling it out for fertilizer on the hay and cornfields. Nowadays it's called organic farming. Back then, we just called it cleaning the barn. It was heavy work: dusty, hot and nasty. After a few hours, my eyes, nose and face were coated; dirt and stink contaminated my clothes; my boots were caked with it; and sweat was running down my neck, chest and back. My arms, legs and shoulders were on fire with pain, but all I could do was clench my teeth, spit and keep on shoveling, until Mr. Brickman said, "Let's go get some lunch."

He didn't have to say it twice. I dropped my square pointed shovel like it was on fire. We coughed, and spit, and blew our noses to the side with our fingers, all the way up to the house.

We dipped basins of water at the stock tank by the windmill and washed up with a bar of brown soap Mrs. Brickman left out for us. I slapped myself half stupid with my hat, trying to knock the dust and the smell out of my clothes. Then we went up to the porch where she was putting our lunch dishes out.

"Hungry Jamey?'

"Yes, Ma'am."

"I know Morrie's been working you like he'll never see you again. You both look like you just crawled out of a coal mine."

"You should'a seen us before we washed up," Mr. Brickman said with a smile.

"Grab a place to sit, Jamey. Don't be bashful."

I sat in one of the kitchen chairs at the little table she'd set. Then I drank a whole glass of ice water that was waiting beside a tin plate, fork and knife. Mrs. Brickman poured it full again from a pitcher she'd just brought out, and then did the same for her husband, who patted her on the leg as she stood there.

"I've got ice tea coming too."

"What's for dinner and where's the kids?"

"They took sandwiches and bottles of pop, and went to pick wildflowers. We're having hamburger steaks and mashed potatoes with gravy."

My mouth started watering as soon as she said it. I knew it'd be real beef, not ground up deer meat. I saw a frown of worry pass over Mr.

Brickman's eyes and face for a moment before he said, "You tell them not to go down by the creek?"

She nodded and disappeared into the house. I sat staring out at the pasture, watching Duffy with his head down in the grass. I can still remember the cool breezes of that late spring day, smelling the purple lilacs blooming next to the porch where we sat. I had no idea it was going to be my last peaceful moment for a long, long time . . . or the very last minutes of what would be called my childhood.

No idea at all.

Ten

Dinner, as lunch was called back then, came between breakfast and supper. It was usually a big meal . . . fuel for the heavy afternoon work still to come.

I was worn out from the morning of shoveling, but reviving in a hurry eating Mrs. Brickman's cooking. It was a far cry from what I was used to, and I ate like a prize purebred being groomed for the state fair. Mr. Brickman however, seemed to have a lot on his mind. I thought maybe he was kind of worn out from the morning's work, him being an old guy in his forties and all, so there wasn't a lot of chitchat at the table.

After I'd hogged down all the meat, canned peas and mashed spuds I could handle, Mrs. Brickman brought out some warm peach cobbler and cream; I groaned and did my manly best . . . eating all of it, right down to the last spoonful. I sat, happy and well-fed, thinking I was ready for what the afternoon would bring. I wasn't. Still a child, I had no idea how cruel and vicious the world could be, but I was going to find out. I was about to become a man. The hard way.

When we had finished our food, Mrs. Brickman started to clear the table. Her husband put his hand on her arm.

"Wait a bit, Sadie? I want you to hear this." He turned to me and said "Tell us about the guy you saw last week. The one was camped out by the bridge."

"A traveling man?"

"Yes, Ma'am. He looks harmless though. Ma and I stopped on the way home. The truck was boiling over a little, and I had to put water in it. Ma called him a whim-wham man. On account of he was selling little statues he'd carved out of pieces of wood. They're good. So good, they look like they're alive. Ma bought a handful, and he gave me and the girls one each."

"Why'd you think he's harmless?"

"He looks retarded, doesn't talk much. When we stopped, he was playing a guitar with a drumstick. The guitar was all out of tune and missing a string."

"Like a turkey drumstick?"

"No, ma'am. Like rat-a-tat-tat. That kind of drumstick."

"Oh, I see."

I think she was embarrassed; her cheeks got pink. Mr. Brickman patted her arm and smiled at her. Then he turned back to me. "You said you saw a couple of campfires this morning."

"Yessir, I did. There was smoke, trailing up on each end of the bend, where all the trees grow."

"Not down by the bridge?"

"No, these were two new ones."

"So there's three of 'em now?"

"I guess so."

No one spoke for a few moments. I could hear the creaking of the windmill as it pumped water into the stock tank at the pasture's edge, and the whistle of a far-off train as it approached Husted. Hot and tired from the long pull up out from Colorado Springs, it was signaling for the pusher engines that would help it up and over the Palmer Divide: the highest point on the Denver & Rio Grande Railroad between Pueblo, the rail and steel mill town to the south, and Denver, "The Queen City of the Plains," sixty miles north.

Eleven

Mr. Brickman was staring off into space, thinking. He looked at his wife, and patted her hand again. Then he said to me, "Grab your hat son, and your saddle. Whistle up that pony; it's time to get to work."

I left my saddlebags on the porch railing after I took out an apple and a piece of sugar. When I unlatched the pasture gate and whistled through my front teeth, Duffy picked up his head, then trotted over to where I stood waiting with the saddle upside down over my left shoulder. I rewarded him with the apple, and he crunched on it while I put his gear on, cinched it, slipped in the bit and looped the bridle and reins over his head. I led him out of the pasture, closed the gate and swung up on his back. I rode up to the house, where Mr. Brickman was just getting out of a green pickup truck.

"I want you to ride ahead of me, point out where you saw the campfires this morning."

"Sure."

I started to ride out.

"Wait a minute."

I made myself comfortable with my right leg up on the saddle horn and watched as he went into the house, returning a few minutes later with a wicked-looking, short double-barreled shotgun. I had heard about them, but never seen one before, except in the movies. I must have stared at it because Mr. Brickman said, "It's a ten-gauge, to keep the foxes and coyotes out of the chicken houses."

I just shrugged, and put my leg back into the stirrup. Mrs. Brickman came out and said, "Morrie, this isn't a good idea."

He didn't say anything, got in the pickup and shut the door. He rolled the window down and leaned out. "When the girls show up, keep them here. I want to see them."

She didn't answer, just stood in the doorway watching as her husband started the truck and motioned at me to move out. I hupped Duffy with my heels and headed back to the trail that led toward home. I could hear the growl of the Ford truck as it moved along behind me in low gear, while the horse pranced toward the creek . . . where an unknown destiny waited for all of us.

Twelve

Duffy wanted to run. I was holding him back as he chewed the bit, sawing his head up and down trying to break into a gallop through the endless expanse of grass.

Mr. Brickman called out the window, "Let him go some."

I leaned forward, almost standing up, and gave Duffy his head. He squatted, then went into a full gallop that nearly tore my hat off. After he had covered the better part of a mile, I reined him in and turned back toward Mr. Brickman. He was even with the second campsite I'd seen that morning. When he got closer, I rode up to his window.

"One of the campfires was down there, where the three big cottonwoods are. I don't see any smoke now though."

"Okay. I'm going to pull over there, you stay by the truck."

He stopped, about twenty-five feet from the trees that grew a little ways up from the creek and shut the engine off. I could hear something ticking under the hood, and feel the heat coming off it as Mr. Brickman climbed out and started for the camp, holding the ten-gauge with both hands. He disappeared behind the trees while I strained to see and hear what was going on. I was standing up in the stirrups when he said, "Jamey, down here," in a loud voice.

I rode among the old cottonwood trees that grew on both sides of the ravine. I could see the highway and the railroad tracks where they ran alongside the creek before they crossed and recrossed each other to the south of us. Mr. Brickman was standing next to a big drift log, looking at the remains of a campfire. Broken whiskey bottles, tin cans, an old shoe, garbage, bones, a piece of what looked like a shirt and a pair of filthy denim pants with the knees and the seat torn out were scattered around the area, like leftovers from an ogre's picnic.

"Damn!" Mr. Brickman said, "they sure left a mess."

"Looks like they cleared out in a hurry too; there's some canned goods over yonder by those rocks." I pointed. We poked around for awhile, checking the brush, but didn't find anything. Mr. Brickman said, "Let's go see the other one."

When we got there, the first campsite was smaller but just as messy, just as empty, abandoned just as fast by the look of things.

"Something sure spooked 'em. Looks like they were fixing to settle in, rest a spell."

I didn't say anything; it looked like that to me, too. I felt my gut tighten as I got an uneasy feeling. Mr. Brickman must have felt something as well. He held the shotgun with two hands, his right thumb laid across both hammers, ready to cock them in an instant. He turned a half circle . . . looking in all directions, but neither he, nor I, could see anything out of place. Even though we couldn't see a thing, I knew somehow . . . that something had happened down here somewhere. Something bad.

"Jamey, when we were having dinner, you remember hearing that train whistle?"

"Yessir."

"Was it northbound? Or south?"

"It was north. The engineers always blow a long note, then a couple short ones, let the helper crews know they're only two-three minutes out, so they'll be ready. The northbound will keep on going and the helper will come up in back of the caboose and start pushing."

Mr. Brickman pulled out his pocket watch, checking. "It's near two hours ago. I'd guess they made it to Denver by now."

I nodded, watched as a frown creased his face.

"Reckon so, unless they had to pull over somewhere, Larkspur or Castle Rock maybe. Let a Pullman through; passenger trains always take the right-of-way."

Mr. Brickman seemed to come to a decision. He snapped the watch case closed and started walking up the stream to the north. I followed him.

After a quarter mile or so, we came to a spot where a couple of section hands for the railroad were checking the bridging of one of the many spans the D&RG had built to cross all of the ravines, gulleys and ditches along the miles of the right-of-way. They were keeping a wary eye on both of us, and the scattergun in Mr. Brickman's hands. He made sure to hold it in a non-threatening way when he called up to the workmen.

"Afternoon, gents. My place is south of here a little ways. There were a couple of fires going along the creek when my hand here rode in around sunup. We're checking for traveling men, but it looks like they cleared out in a hurry."

I didn't recognize either one of the section men, but that wasn't unusual. Sometimes the railroad would send crews from another town, so they wouldn't have to hire and train any new ones. The men who ran the railroad were cheap . . . always looking to squeeze a dollar or two more profit. One guy was pretty big, the heavy lifter of the pair. He looked at the smaller man, who said, "We come down from Castle Rock this morning," he pointed with his left thumb at the two-man handcar sitting next to the tracks, "checking the bridges. We're suppose to go all the way down to the yards in Colorado Springs before we quit tonight. Ain't seen nothing I'd call unusual, 'cepting about ten or fifteen riders on the northbound freight a couple of hours ago."

The man had a wad of chaw packed in his right cheek. After speaking, he half-turned and spit a brown stream. "S'cuze me. Nasty stuff, the tobacco habit. Wife won't abide me doin' it t'home."

Mr. Brickman nodded and said, "You call the railroad bulls?"

"Not yet, figured on doin' it when we get to the yards down yonder."

He pointed with his chin in the direction of Colorado Springs. He went on, "Don't do no good though. They jump off before they get to town, wait 'til dark and hop another train."

Mr. Brickman nodded, whether in agreement or disgust, I couldn't tell.

"Thanks anyway, sorry to bother."

He motioned to me, turned around to head back the way we came. Then he turned again, like he just thought of something more.

"We're also looking for two little girls, eleven and twelve years old. You seen them?"

"Yours?"

"One of 'em."

"Got five of my own, three girls. But sorry. No. We ain't seen 'em."

"You do, tell 'em to get to the house."

"I will mister, I most surely will."

Mr. Brickman nodded his thanks, and stepped off in a quick march, holding the ten-gauge at port arms with both hands. I clucked to Duffy and we followed at a fast walk. Fueled by equal parts apprehension and nervous anticipation, I kept my head on a swivel, my eyes checking every nook and cranny, searching every boulder, tree and the spaces in-between for anything unusual, anything out of place . . . anything wrong. It was a fruitless effort, as we headed south.

Thirteen

We got to the smaller camp and climbed the bank to where the truck was parked. Mr. Brickman turned and looked up at me.

"I'm going to the house, see if the girls have showed up, and call the railroad. I don't think there's any bums still down there, but I want you to ride along the bank, see if you spot any more of 'em."

He looked away for a moment, then back at me.

"I'm gonna give you the shotgun, you see something, shoot a round in the air, I'll come running. Think you can handle that?"

"Sure."

"Don't try to be the Lone Ranger, either. Stay on the horse and keep to the bank. You see more men down there, you signal with a shot. You understand?"

"Yessir. I do."

"Okay. I don't think they're still around, but I want you to check all the way down past the wood bridge."

He handed the shotgun to me and I laid it across the saddle with the barrels pointed away from him. Mr. Brickman reached in his pants pocket and extracted two more fat red-and-brass shells.

"Here, take these. Don't forget what I said."

I put the shells behind my belt, to the right of the buckle, and watched as the pickup disappeared in the grass, heading in the direction of the house. Mister Brickman's property was in the shape of a backward capital letter "L", encompassing several sections of land. The long side was thin and ran north-south; the base thick and fat, went east-west. Lucky for him-it's where the coal was buried and the True-West coal Company had their mine. The thin end was below Husted and notched into the corner of our place. The Brickman house was up in the middle of the dogleg, or elbow as some called it. The house was on higher ground, where the ponderosa pines grew tall and thick. The ranch was about two-thirds grassland and one-third woods, all on the rolling land that rose up into the front range of the Rocky Mountains, and the whole thing straddled Monument Creek. Many ranchers held that Brickmans Flying B Ranch was one of the prettiest spreads in the state, and I found nothing to argue with them about.

I was about a mile from the notch, up on the north end. I reckoned I had two and a half miles down to the south end where the Whim-Wham man was three days ago. I tapped Duffy's flank with my heels and started out. I guided him with my knees, holding the sawed-off shotgun in both hands feeling as deadly as Doc Holliday, heading for the O.K. corral. It was the last-time I can remember feeling so good about the world and my small place in it.

Fourteen

This next part now . . .

This next part, even with the intervention of a World War and twenty years of living, this next part still delivers me tears when I think on it. I see it in my minds eye, as if it were yesterday, and I cannot even now abide the memory . . . it's anathema . . . an abomination hacked up from hell itself.

I rode Duffy at a walk along the high west bank of Monument Creek. The stream had dug itself down about twenty feet in the sandy red soil beneath the grassland, so it was easy to see that there were no railroad bums down there. After what I guessed was about a mile, the trees and scrub brush got thick; the creek had eroded deeper, and the water reversed back and forth several times as the elevation of the land declined, making one last long sweeping turn before it headed south to Colorado Springs and eventually, the Gulf of Mexico.

I wasn't able to see much. A whole tribe of savages could have been under such heavy cover for all I knew. I had to get down there. Look closer.

I backtracked a half mile, letting Duffy go at a canter, until I found a place that wasn't so deep and nosed him over the edge. I jerked the reins back, he sat down on his ass and we slid and stumbled some thirty or forty feet down to the creek bottom. Leaning way back, I had the reins in one hand, the other around the forestock of the gun and my feet kicked hard into the stirrups as we made it down. Duffy stood, shook himself like a dog and turned his left eye on me as if to say, *"What was that all about?"* I patted his neck, retrieved the lump of sugar from my front shirt pocket and fed it to him. I rubbed his neck again and said "Good boy" in his ear. He snorted and we headed south along the creek bed looking for something I hadn't yet seen . . . hoping I'd know it if I did. My uneasiness growing like an ulcer in my gut.

We came downstream through the cottonwood trees, the mountain ash and chokecherry bush; where the switchbacks ran east and west, the grassland retreated and the walls narrowed while the canyon deepened. Duffy took his time, picking his way through the sand and rocks as sure-footed as a mule deer, until we came to where the big bend started. There, it was flat, and wide, and shallow. There I saw a small deserted camp, a couple of empty pint-whiskey bottles and a half-eaten can of pork 'n' beans. I dismounted and scuffed the fire-black circle with the toe of my boot. The last gray ashes and charcoal were still showing some heat. The place was abandoned like the others, within the last couple of hours. I could feel the hairs on my neck and arms stand up as a chill ran down my between my shoulders. I held the shotgun in both hands, gripping it so tight my fingers were cramping. I turned in a half, then a slow full circle, looking hard and careful, my fingers close to both triggers.

Then, the world stopped as I looked across the shallow creek and saw the field of blue and purple columbines blooming over there. I saw something else too. Something that made my breath go shallow and fast, made my heart pound like a steam hammer trying to beat a hole in my chest . . . a piece of lavender cloth was snagged in the driftwood roots of a downed tree. It looked ragged, torn, stained. It was the exact same color as the dress Catherine was wearing that morning, when I swung her up behind me so she could come and visit her very best friend, Maddie. I ran through the water like a mad beast, howling like I'd lost my mind.

Fifteen

I found her where she was left, discarded like yesterday's laundry, her small naked body curled up in a crouch, as if trying to ward off further insult. Her hands were curled into fists. Her body, mute testimony to the violence perpetrated on it, was battered and bruised, stabbed dozens of times in her chest and around her small nipples and unformed breasts, slashed and covered in blood, her innocence ripped away in the most brutal manner imaginable, by a vicious and depraved subhuman beast. She had even bitten through her bottom lip in her agony.

I dropped the gun, falling to my knees in the sand beside her. I cradled her in my arms, trying to comfort the lifeless little body, rocking, endlessly rocking, on my knees, whispering in her ear.

Time stopped. My life changed in that instant and something . . . some elemental piece of me broke. I knew somehow I'd never be the same again. My little sister, the person I'd loved and protected since she was born, was dead. Butchered by a monster. I vowed revenge.

No tears came. I felt a dull ache in my chest and a burning in my guts

51

as I took off my shirt and wrapped the small body in it. I stood, picked up the shotgun and wiped the sand off with my undershirt. I pulled both hammers to full cock and touched off both barrels with a crack and boom loud enough to wake the guardians at heaven's gate. I broke open the breech, ejected the smoking casings, tamped in two fresh ones. As it made a metallic snick indicating the breech had locked, I screamed out: "Beware you sons of bitches; I'll never quit hunting you, not as long as I live! Never."

Then I stepped into the brush and vomited up everything I'd eaten for three days. I puked until I was spitting green bile. Exhausted, I crouched on my hands and knees, still retching . . . gasping for air. When I finally was able to move, I crawled to the creek, rinsed my mouth at the stream and tried to swallow some water to cool my throat . . . and erase the taste of horror lodged there. I picked Catherine up. Cradling her body and the gun, I walked back through the stream to where Duffy waited. He snorted and backed away at the smell of so much blood, but I talked to him, and managed to grab the reins. I led him over to some rocks, stepped up on them and remounted without losing Catherine or the gun.

With Catherine, small and light as a prayer in my arms, and the shotgun under my left leg, we climbed out of the stream and headed for the Brickmans at a fast trot.

Mr. Brickman met me a half mile from the creek. He could see the burden in my arms from a distance and the green pickup was clearing the ground with all four wheels as he ran over the bumps in his haste to reach me.

We closed the gap. He slid the truck sideways and jumped out before it quit moving. The door flopped open and banged like a shutter in a storm as he came to me, his face a mixture of angst, fear and revulsion.

"God in heaven, who . . ."

"Catherine."

"Oh dear God . . . is she . . ."

I nodded, "Yes."

He reached to take her; I shook my head and said, "Take the gun, so I can get down. It's loaded."

He did so and I dismounted, and started walking to the truck. The horror was starting to sink in with him and he groaned as if mortally wounded, then was racked with gut deep sobs that sounded as if he were dying. And maybe a piece of him did. All I knew was that in just one instant our roles got reversed. It seemed he'd become the boy and me the man.

"Maddie . . ." he croaked.

I shook my head.

"No. Looked a bit, didn't see anything. Needed help, and to bring Catherine out. Didn't figure I wanted to go brush popping alone with just two more shells."

He looked dazed, like he'd heard some but not all of what I'd said.

"Take me to the house."

He nodded and we got in the pickup and started it. Duffy stayed where he was. He watched us go, then put his head down in the meadow grass and started grazing. My face was hammered out of granite. I stared out of the windshield holding the precious little body. I had no words.

Mr. Brickman was the color of old barn wood. He kept choking back tears, worry and grief etching ever-deeper erosions in his face as we bounced through the grass. His breathing was coming in shallow, rapid gasps. I could tell he was coming apart inside, consumed with grief, and worry, and guilt about his own daughter. I felt no grief . . . only stone cold rage, and a burning desire for vengeance.

16

Sixteen

We pulled up on what passed for a lawn; I was right next to the front steps. Mr. Brickman came around to my side and opened the door so I could get out. The few steps up on the porch were longer than a march to the gallows. Mr. Brickman called out as he held the summer door with the mesh screen in it.

"Sadie. Come quick."

"I'm right here," she said, before she saw me . . . and became the second person whose life changed before my eyes when she recognized what I was carrying. She sobbed harder when the bare feet and knees came into her focus.

"Catherine," I said without being asked. "Maddie wasn't there. I'm going back to find her."

"We'll go together," Mr. Brickman said.

I nodded to him, said, "I'll need a blanket for Catherine and a shirt for me."

Without a word Mrs. Brickman left. Mr. Brickman started to say something, but I interrupted him.

"Do you have any more shotgun shells, another gun?"

"A whole box of ten-gauge, less four shells. And I've got my father's old Winchester. It hasn't been fired in years though."

"You ever fire either of them?"

"No."

"When's the last time you shot a gun?"

"When I was fourteen."

"Hit anything?"

"A cottontail. With a twenty-two. I cried. Haven't shot anything since. I don't really like guns. Hell son, this is 1940. We've got laws. We're civilized."

"How civilized you think the son of a bitch who done this is?"

I moved my arms up a little. He didn't answer, looked down at the floor. He was clearing his throat as Mrs. Brickman came back with two blankets, some towels and a shirt.

I said, "Get the rifle and ammo."

As Mr. Brickman looked in my eyes, his were full of grief and angst, maybe even pity; his face was gray, and concern was written all over it. He must have seen something in mine that I didn't know was in them . . . an element of command maybe. I don't know, but control of whatever would happen next now rested with me. And we both knew it.

Tears continued down Mrs. Brickman's face as she removed all the things kept on the dining room table. She spread the blankets and placed a folded towel at one end for a pillow.

"Put her here, Jamey," she said in a quiet voice as she brushed silvery tears from her cheeks with both hands. But tears, as anyone who's suffered heartbreak and anguish knows, have a will of their own, and fresh ones coursed down as fast as the old ones were wiped away.

When I laid Catherine on the table, a choked, moaning, pain-and-bile-coated noise slithered up out of my throat like some kind of monster escaping my guts. My denim work shirt, wrapping her savaged little person, was soaked with blood. My undershirt, as well as my arms and hands were dripping with gore. Mrs. Brickman had her face in her hands and fresh tears were pouring out, as I pulled blanket halves over the battered face and sad body that were the mortal remains of eleven year-old Catherine Mae McGoran . . . my baby sister.

Mrs. Brickman looked at me through a double cataract of fresh sorrow, as I tucked the blanket ends in, making them as secure as I could without a needle and thread.

"I need to wash, put on the fresh shirt."

She nodded and led me back to the kitchen without a word. I pulled off my bloody shirt.

"Where can I put this?"

"Here, in this grocery sack."

Mrs. Brickman put the paper sack on the floor, next to the back door, and got a porcelain dishpan from the nail where it hung on the back porch. She filled it at the kitchen sink, handed me a bar of soap and washrag.

"I'll burn both your shirts out back."

"Will you call Ma . . ? She needs to know. Better call Sheriff Malone, too. There are only a couple of hours of daylight left down in that creek bed, I got to get back out there," I said in a gush of words.

I finished at the sink and put on the borrowed shirt as Mr. Brickman came back with a box of shotgun shells, an octagon-barreled lever-action .30-40 Winchester and six brass cartridges. I took the rifle, opened it and looked in the breech. It was dry, but looked serviceable.

"These are all the bullets I could find."

I took them. Two had green corrosion on them. They were fouled, by oil or water probably.

"These two are no good."

I worked the action several times, making sure it would eject the casings after the gun was fired. The bore was clear and clean but, like the breech, needed oiling. I loaded the four rounds and handed it back to him; but it was plain to see that he was at best indifferent to guns.

"It'll fire if the primer in the other shells is okay," I said, pointing to the two bad bullets. I took the Western Ammunition box, filled my pockets with the fat red shotgun loads. I took most of the box.

Mrs. Brickman was leaning against the drainboard, still weeping and wringing her hands, her eyes red and swollen, "I'll make the calls, and clean her up, put a nightie on her."

There was nothing to say. I picked up my hat, looked at the dining room table, nodded my thanks and headed for the door, Mr. Brickman following.

"Morrie."

He turned and embraced her. She had her arms around his neck, and was whispering through her tears into his ear. I went out the front door. They, like Ma and Pa, were no strangers to hardship and grief, having buried both of their mothers and one of Mrs. Brickman's sisters within the past couple of years . . . as well as one or two infants during the worst years of the Great Depression.

I sat in the truck waiting, busied myself checking the shotgun. I stuck three shells between my belt and dungarees, on each side of the fly buttons, another pair in each of my shirt pockets. It was all I could carry and get to in a hurry. Ten loads of buckshot was more than I could ever hope to get off. And, after what I'd seen, I doubted we'd find any railroad travelers anyway. I waited, trying not to think of Catherine and Maddie . . . found I couldn't think of anything else.

To this very day I can still taste the bile in my mouth when I remember that afternoon, and tears come running to me.

Mr. Brickman came out of the house, gray faced and grim, the rifle clutched in his left hand. He climbed into the truck and started it without a word. We drove out toward the place where I'd found Catherine and left Duffy; where my youth ended and all of our heartaches began.

Seventeen

Duffy picked his head up when he heard the truck. Ears at attention, he watched as we got closer, nickered when I stepped out on the ground and whistled to him, then trotted over to where I stood waiting. I laid the shotgun on the grass, checked the cinch and gathered the reins where they'd been dragging. With the ten-gauge in my right hand, I mounted up and walked Duffy to the truck window where Mr. Brickman was scanning the trees along the creek with binoculars.

"See anything?"

"No."

"You gonna walk or drive?"

"Drive over to the trees and park. I'll walk after that."

"Good. I'll cross the creek and come down the far side. You chamber a round in the rifle?"

He shook his head.

"Let me have it."

He passed the rifle to me with the business end pointed at the ground, making it plain he didn't like guns. I stuck the scattergun under my leg, and took the Winchester. I levered the action, watching as a dull brass cartridge slid into the barrel. I closed the breech with a snick. The action felt tight. *Good so far*, I thought.

"Easy Duffy," I said, "easy boy," and snapped off a shot into the trees, aiming at a big cottonwood. The horse jumped a little, but didn't bolt. I worked the lever forward, which flipped the smoking casing out, then pulled it back again, loading another live one. I eased the hammer to half-cock.

"We know it'll shoot now," I said as I handed the rifle back. "Three shots left. One's in the chamber. Don't forget to pull the hammer back."

"I won't," he said as he pressed the starter and the V-eight motor rumbled to life. I tipped my hat and gave Duffy a nudge. We headed back to the creek with its heavy brush camouflage and unknowable, sinister secrets. We splashed over to the far side. I saw Mr. Brickman come down the bank. He began searching the bushes, tree falls and clumps of boulders on the west side. Riding back and forth in a zigzag through the trees and chokecherry bushes, I started doing the same on the east side, in the failing light of the worst day of our lives.

Eighteen

I found Maddie about half a mile downstream, just as the lengthening shadows from the setting sun were sucking the last bits of light from the creek bottom. She was lying on her back, her dress hiked up near her face, legs in an obscene position. Her thighs were bruised and bloody, and one looked dislocated from the savage and repeated rape she'd endured. She was covered in congealed gore from being stabbed and slashed over and over, and from the way her head was bent, her neck looked broken. Like Catherine, Maddie had also bitten through her bottom lip; but I saw one difference: Maddie had a big clump of her silvery blonde hair in her left hand. *She must have pulled it out during her ordeal,* flashed through my mind like a hot steel screwdriver. It was the second saddest sight I'd seen that day, and raised a rage in me that has never left.

The light was gone from what were once bright blue eyes. Only a few hours before, they were filled with light and laughter: the emblem of youth, health and innocence. Now, dull and occluded marbles, they stared without seeing at the base of the scrub oak she was under. Fighting the need to throw up again, I straightened her head and closed her eyes. Then, after getting her legs and feet together, I pulled her dress down, allowing her a small modesty in death. I did it too, to spare Mr. Brickman the tiniest bit of the pain I was about to shower down on him.

Hating what I was about to do, the action I was being forced into by fate, I braced up, cupped my hands around my mouth and called across the creek to him. Others had joined the search in the past few hours. I didn't want to alert them just yet, so Mr. Brickman could have a few moments alone. When I had his attention I waved him over. He splashed through the water at a dead run.

When he reached me, the look of dread on both of our faces said all there was to say . . .

I took the rifle from him, pointed to the place where Maddie was lying.

"Over there. Beneath that scrub oak," I said, adding, "it's bad. Very bad. I'm sorry," but he was already moving toward poor Maddie, a strangled cry of anguish already slipping from his lips. I saw him fall to his knees, grasp her lifeless body to his chest, and bellow out the most awful noise I've ever heard. It was the sound of a still living human heart being crushed . . . and it seemed to go on forever.

Nineteen

The man who stepped out of the kinnikinnick and scrub oak by the streambed, and into the thickening gloom of the coming dark, was a different man from the one who went in. I've never had children, so I can only try to imagine the horror and pain of losing one ... but I don't think a loving parent would ever get over it. And I also believe that Mr. Brickman was a broken man when he emerged carrying the body of his only daughter that day.

He passed me by as if I weren't there, his eyes vacant, walking with the artificial gait of a mechanical man. I think his mind had gone elsewhere; he didn't acknowledge me when I said, "Wait up on top; I'm going for the truck."

He just kept taking those machine-like steps, placing one foot in front of the other, time after time, after time. I got on Duffy, carrying the rifle and cut-down shotgun, and hupped him out of the creek bottom, rode hard and fast for the pickup, two and a half miles upstream.

By the time I drove back to the spot where I'd found Maddie, with

Duffy trotting along behind, Mr. Brickman had carried her some ways out in the grass. He was headed for his house, with the same mechanical steps, the same faraway look in his eyes, and brand-new evidences of grief streaming down his face.

I pulled up in front of him, shut the motor off and got out.

"Mister Brickman."

He didn't pay any attention to me, kept taking those machine-steps into the dying day. Nightfall comes with suddenness in Colorado. The sun touches the mountaintops and is eaten by them, about as fast as you can swallow a lump in your throat. It would be full dark in another few minutes by my reckoning, and I could hear the search parties, other men who'd come by to help, working their way upstream. I needed to let them know there was no longer any need to look; we'd found her. But I had to get Mr. Brickman in the truck first. I stepped in front of him, held him by the biceps.

"Mister Brickman, let me drive you up to the house." I guided him to the pickup truck, opened the door with one hand and he sat, pulled his left leg in, then his right, still clutching Maddie's body to his chest. I rolled the window down, shut the door and said, "I'm going to call the others."

He didn't indicate if he'd heard my words. He just stared ahead, lost in his own nightmare world of small broken bodies and the dead, caressing the bloody rags that only hours before had hugged his neck, kissed his weathered cheek and said in her little girl voice, "I love you Daddy."

I turned the headlights on, retrieved the rifle from the floor and stepped to one side, where I fired off all three rounds in quick succession. The reports were still ringing in my ears and smoke was still slithering out the barrel when the first searcher emerged from the trees along the creek. He came forward, and the others materialized by ones and twos before he was halfway over to where I waited. I met him in the headlights' yellow glow in front of the truck. It was Petey, the cook's helper up at the Hardy House. Before he could ask, I said, "We found her."

"Is she . . . ?"

I shook my head.

"No she ain't."

"Mister Brickman?"

"Takin' it hard. Real hard."

Petey spit out something brown and smelly he'd wadded up between his lower lip and gum.

"It's a sorry son-of-a-bitch of a day."

I nodded, agreeing with him, and said, "I gotta take him up to the house. My pony's done in, and so is Mister Brickman. Why don't you gather the rest and we'll meet up there and figure out what's next."

"Well that sorry-assed sheriff don't figure to be much help. What I hear is he's among the missing today."

The sheriff's bouts of drunkenness were the stuff of legend. Petey added, "That's what y'all get for keepin' the same one in office so damn long."

I nodded at the others, starting to come toward us.

"I'll see alla ya at the house," but Petey'd already stepped away, headed toward the rest of the searchers. I went back to the truck. Mr. Brickman was looking away to somewhere no one else could see. Wet pieces of his broken heart were flooding his eyes and streaming down his face.

Twenty

When we got there, the house was alive with lights and several cars were out front, including our Model-T truck. Pa was there on the porch with two other railroad men, all in their dirty work overalls and denim caps. I could see a bottle of something brown and liquid being passed between grease-stained hands and each of them took a pull before it went over to the next man. I guessed they were pretty well oiled; the red faces and sweaty necks on all three standing there in the porch light giving them away as I wheeled the truck up. I shut the motor off, turned to Mr. Brickman.

"I want you and Maddie to stay here. I'll go clear the way, let the women know we're coming. That be okay with you?"

Tears were still leaving his eyes and traveling down his cheeks. He didn't answer. I got out started up the steps under the staring eyes of three drunks. I looked right in Pa's face and said in a hoarse voice that was grown old in the last few hours, "Make way, and don't none of you say one goddamned word."

It was a voice of authority. With a tone and quality to it that came from the man I was morphing into on that evil day, not the boy I'd started out as, in the early light before dawn. I was bigger than any of them, and had a rage growing inside that could explode into hostility at any moment. They all stepped back, looking down at the floor, and no one spoke as I shouldered my way past.

I caught a snatch of something Pa said to his fellow inebriates as I stepped over, going through the door, about . . . "must've caught rabies or somethin." I couldn't hear what else he said, as the other two laughed. A white-hot rage flared in me, but I choked it off, as all activity in the parlor and kitchen stopped when I came through the door. But one last, stray thought about Pa flashed in my head like the red-and-green neon signs on the gin mills along Colorado Avenue in downtown Colorado Springs. *Laugh while you can,* I thought, *but you have raised your hands to Ma, or me, or any of us, for the last time in your life, you old bastard.*

All eyes in the room were on me when I came through the door, but the first face that swam into focus for me was Ma's. She stood and embraced me with a strength that only a mother in extreme distress could have, as fresh gouts of sorrow erupted from her. The top of her head stopped at my chin, and I smelled her hair as she clung to me. It was as if she was making sure I was real; that I still existed as flesh and bone here in this world. She needed to be reassured.

"I'm okay Ma," I said, "I'm alright. We found Maddie."

Mrs. Brickman, standing behind Ma said, "Is she . . . is she . . ?"

I shook my head a fraction of an inch, "We need a blanket. I came in to get a blanket."

Mrs. Brickman started to collapse, was saved by one of the neighbor ladies and led to an easy chair. Ma let go of me and went to her knees beside Mrs. Brickman, where they hugged each other in mutual sorrow. Someone pressed a red wool blanket which smelt of mothballs in my hands.

"I'm asking all of you to stay here so Mister Brickman can bring her in. Please," I said, "wait. We'll bring her right in."

Twenty One

Pa and his two pals had almost finished their bottle when I went out. Still in the merry stage, he made an exaggerated bow with one hand at his waist and the other, the one choking the whiskey bottle, behind his back. His two companions did the same, all three mocking me together. I went down the steps two at a time.

The search party was arriving in two pickup trucks when I got back to Mr. Brickman. He was struggling, trying to elbow the door handle without releasing the two-handed embrace of his daughter's body. I opened the door for him. He started to work his way out. I said, "Wait. We need to wrap her up." I unfolded the blanket, then laid it across both of them. "Let me have her."

He shook his head, said in a low voice choked with emotion, "No-o-o-o," still trying to get out, to stand up, start for the house.

I poked him in the chest with my right index finger. It must have been a bit harder than I intended; his mouth drew tight and anger flashed across his face. He started to speak, but I cut him off.

"Listen a me. Listen . . . there's a whole damn houseful of people up there, and half a dozen or more searchers out here; Pa and two more railway men are drunk on the front porch. None of them need to see Maddie like this. Now let me have her so we can cover her before you take her inside. Maddie deserves to keep her dignity."

Fresh sobs escaped his chest as he handed his daughter's body to me and together, we wrapped her in a red Hudson's Bay blanket that had a black stripe at one end.

Mr. Brickman sighed and took a deep breath, gathering himself for what he knew was coming next. He took Maddie from me and started toward the house, then turned and looked at me,

"Thank you, Jamey. You did the right thing just now."

"Be right up," was all I could think to say.

He resumed his slow march to the house, his face and eyes set somewhere on a somber middle distance known only to himself, taking careful steps, one after another . . . as if he listened to a funeral dirge only he could hear. I turned to where the searchers were waiting beside a brown Dodge pickup truck.

I nodded to them and took off my cowboy hat, wiped sweat off my forehead with my shirtsleeve.

"Mister Brickman wanted me to let everyone know we found Maddie, and to thank you for your help. He's too sad to talk at the moment, but if you want to come to the house the women have coffee and sandwiches for us. I'll be up as soon as I take care of my horse, he's done in."

"I'll see to him," a voice said, and Petey stepped forward.

"Thanks, I appreciate that but I oughta do it."

"Hell, Jamey, it'd be a favor to me to take care of him. Make me feel like a real cowboy again, instead of a cook's helper."

"I'm too wore out to argue Petey. There's a stall in the barn, water and

74

grain, but don't give him too much. He ate a lotta grass today."

"Don't worry. I done this before, 'sides, that's the smartest horse I ever seen. Smarter than most dogs I know of."

"Thanks, Petey, I'm much obliged."

I untied Duffy from the back of Mr. Brickman's pickup. I rubbed his neck and handed the reins to the lame cowboy. I had a special bond to Duffy; we'd grown up together, and were almost the same age—I'd trained, fed and watered him since I was five years old. As I watched Petey lead him toward the barn, I damn near ran after them, but I didn't. I came to regret it afterward. I turned instead and headed for the house with five other men from the search party, my brain, body and soul numb from the events of the day.

I got to the porch in time to see one of the drunks holding the door open for Mr. Brickman and the sad burden he carried. Mr. Brickman didn't acknowledge the doorman, just turned sideways and stepped over the threshold.

Pa looked to be in the first of his weepy stage. He was sitting on the edge of the steps, with his back against one of the porch posts, nursing a fresh pint of whiskey he'd gotten from somewhere, blubbering to himself about "My poor, beautiful daughter, poor little Catherine . . ." The crying jag would last for a while, depending on how much he'd had to drink . . . and then he'd get mean. Do his best to live up to his Devil-Dog reputation when he was a marine over in Europe during the Great War. The fight would start with whomever was handy, and Ma, me, or his newest bar buddy would be on the wrong end of his anger and his fists while he worked the demons out.

Not ever again, I thought as I followed Mr. Brickman into the house. *You'll never again raise your hand to any of us.*

I took my hat off as I stepped over the threshold, left it behind the door, and the men following after did the same. Conversation ceased. All eyes in the room focused on the blanket-shrouded bundle in Mr. Brickman's arms. Hands moved to faces, subduing gasps, sobs and suppressed wails as everyone in the room broke off a chunk of their heart and crumbled it to pieces in empathy, as every one of them imagined themselves walking in Mr. Brickman's boots. The spirit was sucked right out of the room in less than a heartbeat. Mr. Brickman seemed bewildered all of a sudden . . . like he'd waked from a nightmare and realized a crowd of people stood around him. He turned in a half circle, as if not recognizing his own front room. I stepped alongside, was about to take his arm, when Ma and Mrs. Brickman materialized from somewhere like angels of mercy. They were both devastated; their eyes red and swollen; their faces wet with tears which flowed from a bottomless well of sorrow that only mothers have.

"Please," Mrs. Brickman said. "Please help yourselves to the food while we take care of our babies."

I don't think there was a dry eye in the room other than mine at that point, as the gloom descended on the place like a heavy fog. Ma said, "Come Jamey," and I followed her and the Brickmans as they trooped up the stairs to the bedrooms up there. I went like a blind man, led on by Ma's touch, my anger growing with each sob, each step, each tear . . . the rage burning now like a pint of battery acid in my gut.

I was so intent on Ma's dignity in sorrow, I didn't notice where the Brickmans went, but all of a sudden I was in a spare bedroom where Catherine was laid out. She'd been cleaned up, the blood and the dirt washed away, and she was dressed in the bright blue Sunday dress that was her favorite. With her hair combed and some of Ma's powder to hide the bruises, she looked like she was sleeping. It broke my heart.

Twenty Two

"Jamey, this is our only chance to say good-bye to her in private. We waited as long as we dared to, but the authorities were called a little while ago. The deputy in Colorado Springs said Sheriff Malone wasn't there. He said they'd send some men out with the coroner. It's going to be some time yet, but not too long. I expect they'll ask you about where you found her, and why you moved her."

"I found Maddie, too."

"Mary, Mother of God. What then?"

Trying to spare her, I said, "I called Mister Brickman." I should have known better than to hold information back from her.

"What else then, Jamey?"

"I don't want to say, Ma."

"Best tell me."

"I was trying to make it easier for him . . ." *And you too,* I thought.

Ma's face was drawn, her eyes full of the sadness that was graven into the worry lines etched alongside her eyes and mouth . . . and I realized then . . . that her suffering would last as long as she lived. I put my arms around her, hugged her to my chest and she wept for a long, long while as I held her.

When her pain had eased some, she sat without speaking on a little wood rocking chair next to the bed. I told her an abbreviated, much-sanitized version of finding Catherine and Maddie. She accepted what I told her, even though I think she knew it wasn't the whole truth. It was, however, as much of the whole truth as either of us could handle . . . then or now.

When I finished talking, Ma was quiet. She rocked slightly in the chair with her head back and her eyes closed, as though she were visualizing in her mind, and thinking about what I'd said. Then, she opened her eyes and looked at me, as if she'd come to a decision. Speaking in slow careful words she said, "There's something you should know."

I waited, but she said nothing more.

"What?"

After a long pregnant pause, Ma reached in the pocket of her dress and said, "This was in her hand."

"Catherine's?"

Ma nodded and gave me a small wood carving, about three inches long. It was a manx cat, a lynx maybe, crouched and ready to spring on something smaller than itself. It was made from yellow pine, and about half of it was stained a rusty brown color. It was still a bit sticky and smelled sort of coppery . . . from my sister Catherine's blood.

My world stopped turning on its axis, and I was rooted where I stood, holding the carving. Thoughts of Catherine's and Maddie's last moments on earth flared in my head, while bursts of insight, and finally, the megawatt energy of vengeance coursed through my body as my glands bled gouts of adrenaline. *The Whim-Wham Man, The*

Whim-Wham Man . . . THE GOD DAMNED WHIM-WHAM MAN,
beat an ever-louder tattoo into every cell in my brain, until that name
became my only conscious thought.

I nodded to Ma, looked again at my ravaged little sister, headed
for the door with the Whim-Wham man's countenance dead center of
the gunsight in my mind's eye. Ma watched in silence as I turned and
left. Her face and eyes looked cast in bronze as fresh rivulets of sorrow
and grief coursed down her cheeks and dripped on her breasts. I went
down the stairs two at a time. I went, as a paladin of tortured, savaged
and destroyed little girls. I was a knight-errant . . . the self-appointed
instrument of vengeance for the innocent, the meek and the dead.

Twenty Three

Incandescent with rage, imagining the ways I'd take my revenge when I caught up with the Whim-Wham man, I shouldered my way through the crowd downstairs, making for the front door, without a word to anyone. I bolted over the porch, took the stoop in two jumps and bumped into Petey, coming up from the barn. He reached out, and touched my shoulder.

"Where to, Jamey?"

"I know who done it."

"Sure enough?"

"Yeah. Catherine had it in her hand."

"Had what in her hand?"

"The proof," I said, and opened my fist, the one with the carving Ma had given me, the one with blood on it.

"I don't get it. What's it prove?"

I stared into Petey's eyes for a few long hard seconds. I said, "It proves where she was, the last person she encountered . . . before she was attacked and butchered. Her and Maddie. I call him the Whim-Wham man. Makes carvings and sells them. I recognize his work."

"You're certain of it?"

"Dead certain. Don't ask again."

Petey let go of my shirt. And then he said something I've thought about at least a thousand times in the years since.

He said, "It's a hard, hard road you're about to set foot on, son. Think on it afore you do. Because once you're on it, you can't never get off."

I heard the words, but I didn't pay attention to anything. I was fifteen years old and I didn't pay attention to what they meant; I didn't stop to think . . . and I've paid the price ever since.

But the plain fact is, on that spring night, I was in the jaws of a demon named retribution; and his hold on me was so strong hell itself could not have loosed his teeth.

I left Petey standing there and headed to the pickup truck, where the ten-gauge shotgun was singing a siren song that my ears alone could hear. It was almost like a lover's caress when I reached under the seat and touched the warm wood and cold steel that waited there. I checked the load and shut the breech with a snap that sounded like a breaking bone. I laid the gun next to me as I started the motor.

Because cars and trucks were parked all around the driveway, I had to ease down by the barn in order to turn around. As I started back past the house, Petey stepped in front of the truck with several men. When I stopped, he climbed in the cab with me. The others got in the back, and sat on the edge of the bed. There were five of them counting Petey, and they had lanterns or other gear.

"We're goin' with you."

"So I see. You sure alla ya want to?"

"Yep."

I got busy driving while Petey busied himself rolling and lighting a cigarette from a pouch of Bugler tobacco he carried in his shirt pocket.

"He's got a camp down by the wood bridge, where everything crosses."

"Near the railroad tracks?"

"Yeah."

"The traveling men and the bums been down there long as I can remember."

I didn't say anything for a while. All I could think about was the Whim-Wham man . . . what he'd done to Catherine and Maddie . . . and what I was gonna do when I caught up with him.

It took almost no time before we were close to the place where I'd seen the Whim-Wham man a couple of days earlier.

"Turn off your lights, Jamey, kick it up into neutral and shut the motor off. Coast up there, real smooth and quiet."

"You done this before?"

Petey took a deep drag off of his cigarette before he answered. In the darkness the glow from it lit up his face, giving him an evil aspect, like when you finally get a glimpse of the wolf man at the movies. He blew smoke out of his nose and mouth like a dragon and said, "Yeah. A coupla times. Down in Florida, where I was raised and learnt to be a cowboy."

I didn't want to know any more; I worked the controls and Mr. Brickman's pickup glided in for a quiet stop. The camp was where I remembered . . . its lone occupant still in residence. The Whim-Wham man was about to answer for the butchery of two innocent little girls. I came to a full stop, pulled back on the brake lever and we all got out.

Twenty Four

I went first, holding the sawed-off shotgun at port arms. I was ready to drop my left hand and pull both triggers but I never got the chance. As we crept into the camp, quiet as any six vigilantes anywhere could be, Petey, bad back and all, stepped in front of me as fast and ruthless as a hungry weasel, and kicked the sleeping man with all his might. I heard something snap, a rib maybe with a wet smack that almost sounded like two hands clapping. Squealing, the Whim-Wham man tried to crawl away. Petey kicked him in the stomach and he began to vomit. He was on his hands and knees, retching, when Petey kicked him in the face, and then, he was still.

"He dead?" someone said.

"No."

"How'd you know?"

"'Cause these kind don't never go easy or fast," Petey said, "and they most always cry and beg at the end."

Petey grabbed the unconscious Whim-Wham man by the back of his shirt and dragged him over to where a cottonwood tree was growing, leaving behind a trail of blood, urine and vomit. In a cold rage, I watched as two of our group lifted and pulled both of his arms behind him, and Petey went to work tying the Whim-Wham man's wrists together with a piece of mechanics wire. It was cruel and effective. Then he did the same with his feet, leaving the Whim-Wham man bound to the tree, spread-eagle backward, unable to escape.

Without a word one of the men ransacked the lean-to, while a couple of the others threw all the available wood on the fire. As soon as it started blazing, the meager possessions of the Whim-Wham man went in. It took less than a minute to burn everything he had. What wouldn't burn, like a couple of aluminum pans, were thrown on the blaze anyway, allowing them to melt into blackened unidentifiable lumps. And just like that, in less time than it took to tell the tale, all proof of a living, breathing human life was gone, erased, as if it never existed, from that collective humanity we call society.

The Whim-Wham man regained consciousness when they were about half done. As he lifted his head, I saw a tooth, stuck in the blood and vomit clinging to his beard, as the fluids dribbled down the filthy yellow undershirt he was wearing. He watched with the dull eyes of a stricken beast, as his life went up in flames. It was only when a small box of his carved figures was emptied on the fire that he reacted, shaking his head hard enough to sling spit and blood in all directions. He moaned and struggled so hard against his wire ligature that blood leaked from his wrists, ran down his hands and dripped on the ground.

"Nooooo, Nooooo. I dunow. I dunow. I dunnowoo."

"Don't like it, do ya?" Petey said. "Well it ain't all you ain't gonna like. Not by a long shot. We're here for justice."

I thought about Catherine and Maddie, how they looked when I'd found them, and fresh rivers of disgust, hate and rage coursed through me. My hands shook, my body twitched and my guts felt like a blast furnace as I watched Petey take a pair of worn old leather work gloves from his belt and put them on. His eyes were hot and glittery, filled with hate and something else I couldn't identify as he drew a five-inch hunting knife from the scabbard on his right side. I watched as he stropped the blade on the back of his glove. I heard him say, "You think you can come here? You all think you can violate our children, our women, come here an' kill? And get away with it? You really think that boy?"

Petey's voice got louder, and more shrill with each question, as he went to work with the well-honed, razor-sharp and mirror-bright hunting knife with a staghorn handle. I stood there with four other men and watched in horrific, sickening fascination as a man was being cut up and mutilated. I heard his screams, smelt the blood and the stink of mortal fear on him and watched Petey throw the severed genitalia in the fire. He said, "Just like cuttin' the nuts off of cattle, 'cept cattle don't stink so bad as this'un."

Some of my rage dissipated as the coarseness and brutality of those few shattering, life-altering minutes spun by, so out of control. But there was more to come . . . and it was even worse.

Twenty Five

The Whim-Wham man was crying and moaning. Blood leaked from his ruined face and ran in a stream from his wrecked manhood, dripped in a puddle at his feet. His eyes locked on to mine and never left as Petey looped the piece of rope he'd been using for a belt around his neck and tied a square knot in it. Petey looked around and pointed to an iron bar that had been used as a stake to tie down one end of the lean-to.

"Bring it here."

One of the men pulled it out of the ground and handed it to Petey. He stuck it through the rope and twisted, cutting off the Whim-Wham man's air.

"I dunno I . . ." were the last words the Whim-Wham man managed to speak, as Petey strangled him to death. His face turned red, then purple, and his body quivered as his Adams apple and voice box were crushed by the methodical tightening of the rope. When the hyoid bone in his voice box was crushed, it made a faint but audible sound, like someone cracking his knuckles. His body shuddered in a terrible rictus of death I'll never forget. And then, with his tongue protruding and his eyes bugged out, the Whim-Wham man died.

It was the most awful sight I'd ever seen. Even with all the horrors of that day, and everything that transpired afterward, the death of the Whim-Wham man still brings nightmares every time I fall asleep. The reason? Simple. As he died, his eyes never left mine. He was locked on to my face, as if he were looking into my soul, seeking the answer to his simple, one-word question . . . Why? Why are you doing this to me? Why?

And part of me died too.

I had no answer then, and I have no answer now. But every day, I still see those eyes of his searching my soul as he died, still asking why . . . never getting an answer.

The fire had burnt down, and there was a mounded heap of glowing coals. It was so hot, we couldn't get closer than several feet away from it. I watched with four other stunned men as Petey pulled the steel spike he'd used as a lever from the ligature around the Whim-Wham man's neck. He walked over and threw it in the fire, where it hissed like a dying snake in the coals. He tossed in his hunting knife, the scabbard and his bloody gloves, one by one. They hissed and smoked, then burst into flames and in seconds they were gone. I could see the knife, glowing red, then white-hot as it lay on the coals, then it disappeared into the heart of the fire. Petey said, "I'm goin' to wash my face," and stepped away in the darkness, headed for Monument Creek.

We waited in stone silence, the five of us, staring into the embers, each of us thinking our private thoughts, listening to the rumble and screech of a southbound freight as it slowed, approaching the big turn and wood trestle bridge over the creek. Far off, we heard the moan of a steam whistle and saw the headlight of a north bounder, probably a D&RG Pullman, carting the last passengers of the day up to Denver or Cheyenne, heading toward us.

No one spoke. No one looked anywhere but at the coals as we waited for Petey to come back from the creek and tell us what to do next, all of us thinking, *What Have We Done . . . My God. What. Have. We. Done.*

But Petey didn't come back. And we never saw him again. He'd disappeared.

Twenty Six

The coals were getting a crust of grayish-white ash when I broke the silence, saying, "Maybe he fell or something, I'll go look."

I took one of the barn lanterns and headed down the creek, looking, even though I knew I wouldn't find him.

Behind me, someone said, "See if there's a shovel in the truck. We'd better cut the poor bastard down an' bury him."

I worked my way downstream for a quarter mile or so south of the trestle with no sign of the missing Petey. *Funny*, I thought, *but I don't even remember hearing his last name. I wonder if anyone has . . .*

I got back to the campsite in a hurry. I could see the headlights of three automobiles coming up Nevada Avenue with flashing red lights, and hear the howl of sirens as they came nearer.

The other men had dragged the body of the Whim-Wham man up into the heavy brush of Monument Creek. They were taking turns digging, but it was slow going because of the hardness of the ground, the number of river rocks and the fact that they lacked a pick. The hole was approaching a foot deep when Sheriff Malone stepped into the circle of lantern light. He was red in the face and an oily, smelly drunk sweat poured from his pores as he staggered into our midst. *One of his toadys must have drug him out of whichever place he was whoring, eating and drinking in* flashed incongruently in my mind.

Digging stopped. We all looked at the ground. The sheriff looked at all of us, as if memorizing our faces. He picked up the closest lantern and looked at the Whim-Wham man's body while the five of us stood nailed to our places, wishing to a man that we were elsewhere. Any place elsewhere, and without the deeds of the night tonight on our mortal souls.

Sheriff Malone bent at the waist with his hands on his knees, taking a long close look at the Whim-Wham man's face, the ligature marks on his neck, and last, at his mutilated genitals. He stood with a grunt, and several pops and snaps from his knees and back. He pulled a silver flask from his hip pocket and tipped it straight up. I heard the liquid gurgle and saw his Adam's apple slide up and down as he swallowed. He took a couple of long ones before he lowered his head again. I smelled the raw liquor as he screwed the top back on and wiped his mouth with the back of his left hand. I saw the light, shining off the frame of the big .45 caliber Smith & Wesson revolver he carried on his right hip. He stuck the flask back in his left hip pocket and said, "And which one of yez did this here work?"

"Petey done it," I said.

"Who?"

"Petey."

"Wheresheat?"

"I don't know. He threw everything on the fire and went down to wash 'is face at the creek and he's disappeared. I looked for him all the way down past the wood bridge, he's gone."

"Back up a minute. Wha'd he throw in the fire?"

One of the others spoke up, "He threw the tent spike he used to twist the rope, the knife he used to cut him with, the scabbard the knife was in and, the gloves he was wearing when he done it."

"Then what?"

"Then he said he was gonna wash off, but he disappeared."

"How long ago?"

"Couple of hours. There was a southbound freight."

"And a northbound Pullman."

"Anybody know his last name? Where he lives?"

"Lives up in Palmer Lake. He washes dishes at the Hardy House and helps Tony, the cook."

"How long's he been there?" The sheriff said.

"Coupla years, maybe three, he just showed up one day, looking for a job to do for a meal. Probably hopped off the train," another man said.

"How'd you know all that?"

"It's a small town. I live up there."

We all stood in a nervous bunch, and watched as the sheriff took a cigar out of his shirt pocket. He unwrapped the cellophane and threw it at his feet. He bit the tip off and spit it over to one side. He took a kitchen match out of his jacket and struck it on his pant leg. He lit the cigar, being careful to rotate it around for an even burn. He took a couple of puffs and checked to see that it was well lit, puffed it again, then removed it between his index and middle fingers. He picked a piece of tobacco leaf from his tongue with his other hand, then he said, "One less railroad bum in the world ain't gonna make a whole helluva lotta difference in the great scheme of things. And I know you all got jobs and families to feed." The Sheriff stopped talking and studied his cigar for several long moments. He looked off into the night as he wrestled with his duty and his conscience, torn between choices, between what was legally and morally the right thing to do, and what common sense told him about his record as sheriff and his potential for reelection in the coming campaign. After a few minutes of hesitation and dithering—while the five of us waited with our hearts pounding a fast, heavy and loud tattoo as we envisioned life in prison, or heard in our minds the sound of two pellets of pure cyanide rattling down the chute to an acid bath and oblivion in the form of a lung-searing cloud of poison gas—Sheriff Malone showed his pure politician's heart and soul, choosing his own interests before any other considerations. He looked each of us in the face, as if he was taking a mental picture to remember us by, and said, "One bum more or less don't mean shit to me. He musta hopped back on a train, cause alla yez didn't find nothin' down here." He looked at each of us one last time before he took a last puff on the cigar and threw it in the grave.

He said, "I didn't see nothin' here tonight. But I goddamned-well better see each a yez in the fall, come election time, supportin' me, an' all the rest of our Democrat ticket."

He turned and walked away without another word. I don't think any one of us drew a breath until we heard his car start up and drive away.

Twenty Seven

We dug hard and long that night, and we buried the Whim-Wham man deep, and we rolled big rocks over on top of his grave to keep him there. We didn't talk any and we didn't look at each other as we did it; all of us too scared and ashamed of what we'd seen and done to speak.

It took hours before we finished. We had to make sure the job was done right . . . no one wanted to explain what the coyotes had dug up down there, or what the spring runoff might wash out. The last thing we did was to scout the area for any little pieces of ourselves we might have left behind. We even shoveled up the blood and threw it in the creek, then washed the shovel.

I retrieved the shotgun and unloaded it as we walked back to Mr. Brickman's pickup. As four men climbed up in the bed for the ride back, one of them said, "Wait. Before we get up there, let's make sure we all have our stories straight."

"We looked all up and down the creek and didn't find 'im," another answered.

"What about Petey?"

"What about him?"

"Where is he?"

"We don't know. He left."

"No. Too suspicious."

"He's right. Makes more questions, and not enough answers."

The talk went on like that for a few more minutes with everyone having a word or two, and no one agreeing with the others. Finally, as the world began turning gray with the light from the false dawn before the sun comes up, we hatched a plan of sorts. If someone asked, we'd say that Petey went down to look in a hobo jungle he knew of in Colorado Springs. As excuses go, it wasn't a very good one, but it was all we could come up with. We agreed to keep our traps shut unless asked, and to be as vague as we could with our answers, figuring Petey would get overlooked in the storm of talk about Catherine's and Maddie's murders.

The mention of their names made me ache with a profound grief that dwells in me to this very day. I mourn those two little girls . . . babies really . . . savaged by a monster. A monster that, in a more noble world, would never have drawn its first breath.

I laid the shotgun on the seat next to me, started the truck and turned it around to head back to the ranch house. Nobody wanted to ride in front with me, and a wry smile twisted my lips as I saw the new day's first sunlight leak over the horizon. It looked like the eye of God opening, and it was staring right at me.

The county coroner and Sheriff Malone had taken control of the situation when we got to the house. Most all the neighbors and their automobiles were gone, replaced by the vehicles of the sheriff's men. Over the protests of Ma and Mrs. Brickman, Catherine's and Maddie's bodies had been taken to Glockner Hospital in Colorado Springs for examination and an autopsy to determine the exact cause of death. Afterward, they'd be taken to the funeral parlor down on Nevada Avenue. Funeral arrangements would have to be made and notices put in the newspapers.

The adrenaline surge had left me and I was so tired I could barely move. As I made my way up the porch steps, I noticed an absence of drunks there.

Must have crawled away somewhere to sleep it off or find more whiskey, I thought as I reached for the door. Pa would stay drunk for days on end when he got the urge, and running out of alcohol was the only way he'd quit even then. At least our old flatbed truck was still parked in the yard. I went inside to face the music.

Sheriff Malone questioned me for an hour or two . . . I had no idea of the time . . . about how, where, what time and why I'd moved them after I found Catherine and Maddie. He asked me what I thought happened. I told him about the Whim-Wham man and the carvings he'd made with his jackknife. I told him about the one in Catherine's hand and showed it to him. He asked me about the search; I told him we didn't find anything, that the camp was gone when we got there. He knew I was lying, but didn't press me about it. He just nodded and made a note on the form he was writing. He told me I'd have to come down to his office next to the jail on South Cascade Avenue the next day to sign the statement, after it was typed up. I told him I would, and after a few more questions he was done. The other four men confirmed my story and we all went home.

Twenty Eight

The Brickmans were in seclusion with their grief. Maddie was brought to them late in life, and they'd doted on her from the day she was born. After everyone else had gone, I put the rifle and the shotgun on the kitchen table, along with the keys to the Ford pickup truck. I let Duffy out in the pasture, where he had the freedom to move about and roll around in the grass. He ran out to the middle of it, turned and whinnied to me. Then he pranced further into the grass and put his head down in it. I called after him and said, "I'll be back for you tomorrow."

I cranked the Model T, and Ma drove us home. We didn't say much as I remember; we were both too damn tired for talk. As we pulled up in front of our old house, there was Pa, slouched up on the front steps nursing another bottle of whiskey. His face was beet-red and oily, sweat and grime lined the seams around his nose and down his neck, his eyes were shot through with blood and busted capillaries . . . he looked as mangy, rough and mean as a wounded coyote. And he was spoiling for a fight. As soon as he saw us, he took a last big pull off his bottle and threw it in the flower bed. He wiped his mouth with the back of one hand, stood up, and started down the walk toward us.

Ma was closest to him, sitting in the driver's seat.

"Drive past the walk before you stop, I'm getting out," I said.

Ma, who'd been on the wrong end of Pa's drunken rages before, knew what to expect, but I don't think she had any idea of what was coming next.

I stood on the running board and jumped off as she drove past. I met Pa at the end of the walk. He didn't say one word. He just came at me with a snarl on his face, swinging with both fists, not expecting any resistance, thinking that Ma or I would be his punching bag, like we always had before.

Not this time. Not ever again, I thought as I ducked under his wild, looping swings, and stopped his momentum with a stiff arm to the chest. He made a grunt of surprise, and came at me like a wild man. I was bigger than him, taller and stronger, but he was meaner and crazier. His attack became frenzied and all of a sudden, I was fighting for my life.

That's when all the rage that had melted out of me when the Whim-Wham man died came back. In a red haze of inhuman strength, fueled by anger and adrenaline, I fought back with a crazed energy I didn't know I possessed. I lashed out and connected, followed by two crunching body blows. I heard the air whoosh out of him as his fists rained down on me and I moved toward him, stepping in and following through with body weight and vicious punches to the heart and ribs. He tried to kick me in the balls, missed and went down in a heap. I didn't even realize I was on top of him, beating the living shit out of my pa until Ma finally stopped me, grabbing my arm and screaming at me to quit before I killed him.

I stood, assessing the damage. Pa's face was bloody, his eyes were bleeding. His nose looked broken, and blood was splashed all over his front. His jaw was broken and hanging down, exposing a bloody mouth and gums, and all but one of his front teeth were missing. His lips were swollen and bleeding, and together with the broken jaw, his mouth reminded me of a torn pocket, flapping and hanging down like a rag.

My face was cut over my left eyebrow and my right ear wouldn't stop ringing. One eye had a big mouse under it and my mouth was bleeding from a cut to my lips and cheek. My hands hurt. They were cut and bloody from knocking teeth out, and I was covered in blood from Pa's ruined face.

Both Pa and I had plenty of bruises, cuts and welts to our bodies, but I didn't think anything was broken that couldn't be seen at that point. And that's when Pa decided to take one last shot at being a hard-ass. He moaned, rolled over and made an obscene gesture at me and Ma. I lost it. I hauled off and kicked him in the side with the heel of my boot, as hard as I could. I heard a rib snap like the crack of a whip. Then I staggered in the house, fell on my bunk and slept for sixteen straight hours with all my clothes on.

It was four thirty in the morning when I woke up, sore all over and hoping yesterday was something my brain had choked up from the place where nightmares come from; where monsters live and play; where they dismember and eat the flesh of their barely alive but aware victims . . . hoping, but knowing as soon as I awoke . . . that I was part monster now; that my personal demons, once loosed, could never be fully controlled or incarcerated again. I was sick at my stomach. It felt like I'd been run over by a whole herd of horses. But I found by trial and error that everything still worked as I went out to the privy in my stocking feet. We had electric lights and indoor plumbing by then, but

I was still in the habit of using the outhouse.

Ma was rattling around in her kitchen when I came back. Her face was red and swollen from weeping, and some instinct told me that her load of heartache was going to get heavier. She pulled a chair out from the table and said, "Sit yourself down then, and let me have a look at you Jamey."

I did as she said, finding more bruises and cuts when I lowered myself into the chair. I winced, and took another breath as I came to rest. Ma had washrags and clean towels on the drainboard, and she filled the gray porcelain dishpan with water from the teakettle on the stove. "Take your things off. Down to your skivvies and let me clean those cuts."

Mr. Brickman's shirt was torn and bloody, some of the buttons were gone, and there was ground-in dirt, grass and sweat stains. I peeled off what was left of it, with hands that looked like sausages, swollen and full of deep crescent moon–shaped wounds where I'd connected with teeth. I couldn't undo the buttons on what was left of the sleeves, so finally I ripped them off, heard them hit the floor like the click of animal claws. I dropped the rest of my clothes on top, and began seeing the damage Pa'd inflicted. It wasn't pretty. I heard Ma's breath hiss when she turned and saw me.

It was then I realized, I couldn't see out of my right eye. It was swollen shut. Ma put the basin on the table, got the towels and dishrag and began tending to my wounds. She checked my hair and scalp first . . . then worked her way down.

"Can you see with your right eye?"

"I don't know."

"Try."

I pulled the lids apart, being as gentle as I could, with my fat fingers.

"Yeah."

"Yeah what?"

"I can see."

"No double vision?"

"No."

"Good. Your eye will be fine in a few days when the swelling goes away."

She was cleaning the cut over my left eye when it opened up and started bleeding again. It wouldn't stop.

"Dammit. I'm going to need you to hold this here, Jamey. Press hard."

She guided my hand to the washrag on my brow and left. I held the cloth and waited, thinking about how much my life had changed in the last two days. I stared at the stove, glad for the warmth of the fire, and tried not to think about the Whim-Wham man or vigilantism. It wasn't easy.

Twenty Nine

Ma came back with white adhesive tape, a roll of gauze, iodine, her sewing basket and some other stuff in her apron, put it all on the table.

"I'm going to have to sew you up. It'll hurt some."

I shrugged, watched as she laid her stuff out on a clean towel. She put everything in the order she was going to use it, the last items being a needle and black cotton thread.

"Lean towards me."

I did. She took the towel off. My face leaked blood. She put a glass dropper of iodine on it, which stung. A lot. Fluid trickled out of my eye, but Ma stayed at it. She pinched my eyebrow with her left thumb and index finger, picked up the threaded needle with her right.

"Hold still."

It wasn't as bad as I thought it would be. Ma used a small needle and was nimble with her hands, putting fifteen stitches in to close the wound. Last, she dabbed on more iodine, some petroleum jelly, covered it with gauze and strips of adhesive tape.

"How'd you learn to do all this, Ma?"

She continued with her work and said, "I was still a lass, about your age, when the Rising happened. It was Easter Sunday, 1916, and ours was a Republican house. Mother, my mother, was in service there, and the master was a member of the Irish Republican Army. The house was where some of the wounded came to be treated. I was pressed into assisting when more causalities started coming than Master could treat. He was a doctor. It's when he noticed I wasn't a child any longer. My personal trouble began and I came to America, met your pa."

"How is he?" I was ashamed I hadn't already thought to ask.

"Not so good right now. We need to talk, Jamey. Serious talk."

An icy snake crawled into my guts and coiled itself . . . waiting.

Ma worked her way down my face and shoulder, washing, then tending each of my wounds. Some required more attention than others. She said, "You have five bite marks on your neck and shoulders. These two," she touched my left shoulder and the base of my neck, "are deep. You're going to have to watch them carefully, lest they get infected."

The snake in my guts got bigger, took a grip on my scrotum, made itself comfortable there, and in my guts. "What do you mean? Won't you be here to look at it?" I felt small and afraid; as if I was five years old. "Where's Pa?"

Ma had her back to me, rinsing out a bloody washrag. I could see fresh tears on her face when she turned around. "He's in the hospital. Down in Colorado Springs, and he's in rough condition."

"How rough?"

"He's in the intensive care section."

Ma brushed her cheeks with her wrist and worked on my arms and chest.

"He has two broken ribs and five cracked ones. One of the broken ones punctured and collapsed his right lung. He was coughing up blood last evening. His spleen was ruptured and they removed it. His left eye socket is broken, the doctors won't know for a while if they can save his eye. His jaw is dislocated and broken in several places, they'll put a plate in today and wire it back together, and last, he's missing about half of his teeth."

I looked at Ma, my mouth open in disbelief. I felt like I was about to throw up, and my breath was coming in quick short gasps. The snake had me now from testicles to chest, the icy coils squeezing tighter . . . and tighter.

The bile was rising in my throat when Ma said, "You'd better put your head down, between your knees. Breathe deep. It'll pass."

I did as she said, thinking all the while about monsters; about the one I had loose inside me, wondering how to keep it controlled, worrying about becoming a monster . . . thinking maybe I already had.

I felt better after some deep breaths and sat up. Ma hugged me to her bosom and held me tight for a long moment. I heard the beating of her heart and I felt the shaking of her arms and chest as she sobbed without a sound. I slipped my arms around her and squeezed, wishing she'd never let go.

"There's more, Jamey, and not a lot of time. Finish washing up, here's more water. I'm going to make you some breakfast."

I realized that lunch, the day before yesterday, was the last meal I'd had, and I'd thrown that up. All of a sudden, I was as hungry as a starving refugee.

I got a clean washrag from the pile on the table and said, "Don't look."

"Don't worry, I won't. When you finish, go put clean clothes on, like you're going to school."

I came back in the kitchen a few minutes later to the smell of coffee, frying eggs and bacon. The table had a plate, a knife and a fork set out, a glass of milk, jam and cold biscuits. I had on my best boots and dungarees, a tooled leather belt with an oval buckle, the blue shirt with slash pockets and snap buttons that Ma bought me for Christmas. I sat, and dove in the jam and biscuits, eating all three of them and drinking the glass of milk while Ma cooked. I watched her, waiting for her to speak. When she did, I felt the weight of the whole world come down on me.

 Thirty

Ma brought food, a lot of food. She'd fried eggs, bacon, potatoes and onions and a big stack of hotcakes. She put the food on the table, then got the enamel coffee pot and two chipped china mugs. She poured coffee for both of us and sat across from me. She didn't waste time.

"Jamey, you are the light of my life, but you've got to go."

Her words didn't register at first. I had a strip of hotcake, with a piece of egg and some bacon rolled up in it on the end of my fork and halfway to my open mouth before it did. I set the load back on the plate and looked up. I saw a new fountain of tears watering Ma's cheeks and tracking down her old flannel bathrobe.

"What . . . how? Where? Why?" all came out of my mouth in a rush, like thunder during a summer cloudburst.

Ma put her right hand on mine, it was warm, hot almost, and I could feel her rough skin, callused and cracked from incessant work.

"Please Jamey, eat. There's not much time. I'll talk. You eat and listen."

I picked up the fork, forced it in my mouth and chewed, but I wasn't hungry. My appetite was gone, replaced by a feeling I can only describe as being like falling from a great height . . . and waiting for the impact.

"I couldn't stand to lose you, Jamey. Losing Catherine has left a hole in my heart, that won't ever heal. I'm trying not to think about it too hard right now or I'll go to pieces. I learned during The Rising that the only way to get through is to concentrate on one thing at a time or go mad. I'll grieve later . . . If something happened to you, were you to die I don't think I could go on."

"I ain't gonna die, Ma."

"You don't know your pa. He's sick, sick in the head."

"He always gets mean when he gets drunk. He's always hitting one of us."

"You eat."

"I'm trying."

"Your pa is sick in the head from the war. He was gassed. Mustard gas they called it because it was a pus-yellow in color and smelled like mustard. The Germans started using poison gas when the armies were stalemated in the trenches in northeast France. Mustard gas is thick, and oily, and it puts blisters on the skin, and attacks the lungs. In your pa's case it's affecting his brain. After the whipping you gave him, I'm afraid he'll try to come after you with a gun or a knife, or something, because he knows that in any kind of fair fight you'll win. He can't stand the thought of that. I'm sure he'll come after you the first chance he gets."

My appetite was gone. I pushed the half-eaten plate of food away from me. Stunned, I sat up in my chair and looked at Ma, felt the planet tilting beneath me. Across the table, Ma looked as devastated as I felt. I said, "Where am I going to go?" My throat so tight my voice cracked and I croaked, like an old, smoky, whiskey-drinking cowboy who'd spent his lifetime in the sun and the wind and the elements.

Ma said, "I've been thinking about that since Dr. Gremillion took your pa and Annie down to the hospital in the springs. I th . . ."

"What's the matter with Annie?" I hadn't even thought about my littlest sister.

"Dr. Gremillion thinks she may have scarlet fever."

"What's that? Is she gonna die?"

"No, most likely not. But she'll need special care and treatment. It has to do with her heart; scarlet fever does something to the heart, and weakens it."

The anger-monster inside me came to life for a moment then curled up and went dormant again, as if letting me know it was still there . . . ready to snarl back into action in an instant.

"I'll take care of her, Jamey. She'll be fine; she's tough in her own way. Right now you're my biggest worry. I've got a cousin I want you to go to. He's got a little farm in upstate New York, at a place called Neversink. I've written him a letter of introduction for you. His name is Dennis Harrigan; he's my great aunt Mary's son. Their family came over during the famine, back in forty-seven. Worked on the big canal back there, fought for the Union in the American Civil War. Dennis was over there, in the Great War, same as your pa."

I thought about what she was saying. "How come I've never heard of Dennis Harrigan? Or upstate New York before?"

Ma looked at her hands, now folded together on her lap. After a long moment she looked at me and said, "Because it's where I'd planned on escaping to with you and your sisters, if or when things got too bad with your father."

It felt like I'd been hit with a bucket of cold water. I took a couple of deep breaths and looked at the floor of the kitchen, saw the holes in the linoleum where it had been worn out for as long as I could remember, saw the shelf on the wall with no paint, the broken, chipped, and cracked cups and plates where they'd been washed and dried and stacked . . . and felt despair for the first time in my young life.

Ma pulled two white envelopes from her bathrobe pocket and pushed them over the table to me. "Take these."

"Why?"

"One is a letter to your uncle Dennis. The other is the money I've saved to leave with."

"No, Ma. I can't."

"There's no time to argue, Jamey. You need to be at the Hardy House in Palmer Lake before the early Pullman comes through. Take it to Denver and get on the Zephyr going east. Make connections to New York. It's all there with the money. Eat cheap. You don't have any extra. Dennis will help you once you get to New York."

"Why Palmer Lake?"

"I don't want too many people seeing you go."

"Ma, I don't want to go. I can't take the money."

"You have to. Please, do this for me."

"I don't feel right about it."

"I can't lose you too, Jamey. You have to take the money. You have to go. We haven't even talked about the Whim-Wham man yet."

I froze at the sound of his name. "What about him?"

"Not now. No time. But I don't think he was gone."

I'd never lied to her until that moment. "He wasn't there."

She looked at me with her eyebrow arched up. "So you say, then. We've got to go. Take your razor and toothbrush, go and get the truck started. I'll be right out." She pushed the envelopes into my lap and left. I folded them in half, stuck them in my breast pocket, snapped it closed and went to crank the Model T.

I don't remember what was said on the drive up to Palmer Lake . . . or if we said anything at all. I believe it must have been the saddest journey any mother and son took that day. I do remember the eye of God opening up and the light of another day spilling out . . . and I remember feeling like it was looking at me once again. I couldn't keep from thinking about how much my life had changed in just a couple of late spring days. *It's hard to believe that I still see through the same two eyes, and speak with the same tongue, or feel with the same heart.* And somewhere in the back of my brain, the Whim-Wham man was tied hand and foot to a tree, awaiting the hard hand of vigilante justice, and two innocent little girls lay dead in a closed room; victims at the blood-red hands of an uncaring monster.

When we got to Palmer Lake, I turned around and stopped across the street from the Hardy House. The lights were on, and I could see Tony at the cash register behind the counter, talking to a lone customer paying his tab. As I coasted to a stop and set the hand brake, Ma said, "Get yourself to Denver then, and take the train east. It's all in the envelope I gave ye. Write me when ye get there. Don't make a scene; don't tell anyone where ye're going."

"Tony'll know."

"Ye're going to Denver then. That's all. Listen to me, Jamey. I know of what I speak."

Her brogue was thicker than I'd ever heard. I knew her heart was breaking, her family destroyed and knowing somehow that more heartbreak was in her future. I got out and she slid behind the wheel. I leaned in and kissed her cheek, told her I loved her.

"I know," she said, not looking at me. I turned to go and she drove away without looking back. I went across the street on feet and legs made of lead. Down the valley below Husted, I could hear the faint whistle of the early morning train for Denver. With only my anger-monster for company, I'd never felt so alone.

Thirty One

Tony looked up when I walked into the Hardy House. "Jeez son, what happened to you?"

"Got into it with Pa."

He nodded, concern written all over his face. "I'm so sorry to hear about your sister and the other little girl."

I nodded. Said, "I gotta go to Denver, do some things for Ma."

He nodded and stepped over to the ticket window. "You want a round-trip?"

"Better not . . . I don't know how long it's gonna take me to get done. I'll get a ticket up there when I'm finished, catch the next one back."

Tony nodded, stamped the ticket and pushed it over the counter.

As I was paying him with a small bill from Ma's envelope, I said, "Petey get back okay?"

Tony looked out the window for a moment, then back at me. His face was flushed with anger. He took a pack of Luckies out of his shirt pocket and lit one, laid them on the counter, took a deep drag and exhaled before he answered me. "No. And he ain't gonna be back neither, 'less he wants his ass kicked real good an' proper."

I waited for Tony to say more. After another drag or two, he did. "I run him off three days ago. Caught him drilling holes in the wall back where his cot was . . . into the ladies bathroom. He was spyin' on 'em, especially the young 'uns—ten, twelve years old."

A bolt of unease hit and settled into my chest. I heard the Whim-Wham man in my head, *crying I dunno, I dunno, I dunno,* saw the tears and snot running down his face and beard . . . smelled his fear and saw the blood when Petey cut him with his knife. I blinked several times to erase the visions. "He go?"

"Yeah. I stood right there an' watched him put his shit in a seabag. I gave him his wage and he lit out, same's he got here, down the tracks. I had a big two-handed meat cleaver in my hands. He knew not to frig around, knew I'd use it."

"How long was he here? Seemed to me he was always around."

Tony took another Lucky Strike out of the pack, lit it with the stub of the old one. "Two years or so, I guess, why?"

I shrugged. "You ever hear what his last name was?"

"No, come to think of it. In fact, I ain't even sure Petey is his real name. It's just what he told me it was, the day he showed up. He was broke and hungry. I needed a dishwasher, put 'im to work for a meal."

I could see all the smoke from the morning train, now only a couple of miles down the valley. The engine was working hard, pulling up the grade. It would make Palmer Lake in another five minutes. I said, "He was always nice to me."

"Yeah. He loved that horse of yours too. Always swipin' a carrot or something to feed 'im."

"You ever know him to be mean, hurt anybody?"

Tony picked up his cigarettes and stuck them in his pocket before he answered. "I never seen him be mean, no. If you asked me if I thought he could be, then yeah. I do. He was pretty beat up and cut when he first come here. And I never seen him without that Marbles hunting knife strapped on."

"What's a marble knife?"

"Marbles. It's a brand name, like KA-BAR or Keen Kutter. They're kind of expensive. He was proud of it."

"Was it in a tooled leather scabbard? Had a staghorn handle?"

"Yeah. Always wore it on 'is right hip."

I nodded, as if I already knew, thinking, *He didn't seem too upset, when he threw it in the fire* . . . Out loud I said, "Where'd he come from?"

"Don't know. He was headed south when he got here . . . went the same way when he left. That's all I can tell you. Now that I think on it, I worked around him a couple of years, but I don't hardly know nothin' about him. The man talked a lot . . . but he never said much. About himself I mean."

I had Tony make me a ham sandwich, wrapped in wax paper, for dinner. I went to pay him, but he said, "It's on the house. It's the least I can do."

I thanked him, stuck it in my jacket pocket and got on the train. There was an open seat by the window where I sat and stared out, as we humped up and over the Palmer Divide. Worms of doubt started eating holes in my consciousness, while I thought about all of the events of the three days since I'd seen the break of dawn, and Duffy carried me through an endless sea of grass that stretched all the way to beyond the horizion.

Thirty Two

The train wound its way around Greenland, through fields of purple, blue and white columbines. It made stops in Larkspur, Castle Rock and Parker, finally steaming into Union Station in downtown Denver about two and a half hours after it left Palmer Lake. It was nine o'clock in the morning.

I had been wrestling with my conscience the whole trip. Taking Ma's nest egg was wrong. I knew it was wrong in my heart . . . I decided I couldn't do it . . . wouldn't do it. I stepped off the train.

There to greet me was a big poster on the wall of the station. It showed a handsome, strong-looking man standing at attention and shouldering a rifle. He was wearing a dress blue uniform and had a determined look on his face. BE A MAN, it said,

JOIN THE UNITED STATES MARINE CORPS

Underneath the caption was an address for the recruiting station.

I stared at the poster until I saw my own face on it, asked a redcap for directions, walked a few blocks downtown. I found the building and went in.

By the spring of 1940, the world was on fire. The Germans had invaded Poland in September of 1939, Britain and France declared war on Germany and fighting broke out all over Europe. The Brits and the French were being mauled by Hitler's army and were in retreat as I stepped into the recruiting station. Most folks already had an opinion about it: *Let Europe fight its own damn war. Keep our American boys home.* I sighed, and walked up to the desk . . . all set to test that opinion.

The marine behind it wore starched and pressed khakis with a crease in them that looked sharp enough to shave with. He had a sleeve full of stripes and a chest full of ribbons. He wasn't a big man, like I expected, but when he glanced up from his newspaper, his face looked as tempered as a pair of ten-year-old boots and tough as a nine-pound hammer. He inspected me up and down with eyes the color of a March sky and said, "Well damn, boyo. What's the other guy look like?" The name plate on his desk said Gunnery Sgt. Howard Lee Millsap, and he had a west Texas drawl.

"He's in the hospital."

"Gonna live?"

"I guess so?"

"Anybody you know?"

"My Pa."

His eyes ,which had been crinkled with amusement, took on a serious look of concern. "Just how much damage did y'all do?"

I felt my face flush, looked down at the floor before I went ahead and recited the litany of Pa's wounds.

Sergeant Millsap was all business. "What'd ja use on him— a pipe, board, rock, maybe?"

"Just my fists. And I kicked him two or three times."

"That's how his ribs got broke?"

"Maybe. But I hit him there with my fists quite a few times too."

"Show me your hands."

I held them out, palms down. There were tooth marks all over them where I'd cut myself on Pa's face, knocking his teeth out. They were still swollen, and ugly as a train wreck, I wasn't proud of the way they looked, or how I'd got them.

He let go of my hands and sat back in his chair. He looked at me for some moments before he spoke. I could hear the tick of the hand on the electric clock on the wall, just before it moved. Finally he said, "You been charged with anything? By the sheriff or the district attorney? And don't lie to me."

"No, Sergeant, I . . ."

"Gunney. You call me Gunney."

I didn't know at the time that it was a term of respect, as well as rank.

"No, sir," I said playing it safe, "I haven't."

"You have any wounds I can't see? Gunshot, stabs, cut, anything like that?"

"Some bites and scrapes."

"Where?"

I pointed to my left arm and shoulder. "Here."

He said, "Take off your shirt and show me."

I did as he asked. When he saw all the bruises and bite marks, he whistled through his teeth. "Well Jeff Constant and Jesus Holy Christ . . . you look like you been chewed by a fookin' bear."

With two Irish parents, I knew exactly what the verb "to fook" meant. I put my shirt back on and almost smiled to myself.

"And you wanna join the Marine Corps?"

"Yes, sir, I do."

"Well, the corps needs fighting men, and you can damn sure do that. And he's in the hospital you say?"

I nodded, looked down at the floor, said nothing. The Gunney spun his chair off to one side, looking out the window and thinking for a long while, then came to a decision. He opened a drawer and removed a file folder. He took out a fountain pen, removed the cap and selected a form. "Name?"

"Ja . . . Jake McKern."

"Age?"

"Eighteen," I lied.

"Date of birth?"

"February 20, 1922," another lie, but I figured *what the hell . . . in for a penny . . . in for a pound*, as Ma used to say.

Thirty Three

And that's what I did, I joined the United States Marine Corps under an assumed name, and I've been Jake McKern ever since. I even had it legally changed a few years after the war, when I came home with a sleeve full of stripes and a chest full of medals, when some folks called me a hero. But I've never felt like I deserved that, being called a hero, because the real true heroes are the men like Gunnery Sergeant Howard Lee Millsap who was lost . . . as his buddy Jeff Constant had been in the Great War . . . along with a few thousand other good marines, in November of 1943 at a place called Tarawa. It's a tiny little dot in the Pacific Ocean, in the Gilbert Islands, where the Marines waded ashore for five hundred yards under intense enemy fire, because the tide was out, making the lagoon too shallow to permit the LSTs to pass over the reef and get to the beach.

On the afternoon of the day I joined up, I walked to the post office, bought a money order and sent most of Ma's money back to her, along with a letter explaining what I'd done, and why. She was upset at first, and angry with me, but as loving mothers always do, she soon forgave me for disobeying her. In time, I think she understood, and even approved. I sent half of my pay to her every month I was in the corps.

Ma and Pa lost the ranch in January of 1941. There's an old quote, I mentioned before, but it's worth saying again, about a man looking for a reason to drink can always find one. In Pa's case he didn't have to look very hard, neither. He lost his job at the D&RG while he was in the hospital. When he got out, the first thing he did was to get drunk and the next thing he did was kill Duffy . . . to get back at me, I suppose, and he did. He damn sure did. I cried when I got the news from Ma. Pa took my deer rifle and shot him, right there in Mr. Brickman's corral.

Ma left him then. Took little Annie and moved up to Palmer Lake, where she worked for Tony at Petey's old job in the Hardy House. Eventually she ran it when Tony took sick a year or two later. When the Hardy House closed, Ma managed to buy it and turn it into a diner and, later on, an Italian restaurant. It's still there and I go up and have supper with her and Annie at least every other week or so, if I'm not on a case. The last I heard of him, Frank McGoran was just another wino living on skid row, up in Denver. He may even be dead by now. I don't know. And I don't think I care, either.

Mr. and Mrs. Brickman never got over the loss of Madeline-Jean; Maddie as she preferred to be called. Ma wrote me that Maddie and Catherine were laid to rest together, at the Evergreen Cemetery in Colorado Springs. Mr. Brickman paid all expenses for both funerals, with identical caskets and everything. Right after that they moved away. Mr. Brickman sold his ranch to the True-West Coal Company, but kept on getting his royalty payments for the mineral rights. The coal company in turn sold a portion of it to the federal government when the Air Force Academy was built. The portion is where the NCO housing area is now. The ranch, like the settlement of Husted, is part of the Academy and forgotten about today.

Regarding the other characters in the affair, Sheriff Malone was reelected in the fall of 1940 by a landslide. Unfortunately, he died two weeks later of a heart attack. Legend around the department is that he weighed in excess of five hundred pounds. That's the legend, and not his true weight I'm sure, but he was a whopper for certain, and morbidly obese for a fact.

Of the other vigilantes that night, I can only say that one died in Europe during the war. Another died of natural causes a few years ago. The third one lives and works in Washington, D.C., and the fourth is a successful businessman here in the city. Active in politics, he may even be elected to high public office someday.

As for myself, I lied my way into the marines like I said. I spent my sixteenth and seventeenth birthdays with my brothers-in-arms, and on the morning of my eighteenth, August 7, 1942, I waded ashore with the First Marine Division at a place called Guadalcanal. There, I learned the rage-monster still lived inside me, but that with effort I could control and direct it some. Somehow it worked. I came through the war, and four amphibious landings under enemy fire with only minor wounds.

When I got back to Colorado, I finished high school, then went to college up in Fort Collins on the GI Bill. I joined the Colorado Springs Police Department right after, which kept me from being recalled and sent to Korea, and made detective in just six years. I think my war record may have had something to do with that, but I'm not certain. I do know for a fact that my takedown of the Colorado Commercial Bank bandits as they were coming out the front door with guns blazing and bags of money in hand in nineteen fifty-five moved my name to the front of the promotions list. I know this for certain because the chief told me so at the award ceremony, when he pinned a commendation on me. But the truth of the matter is that it was pure luck; I just happened to be in the right place at the right time . . . eating lunch at the Grand Cafe across the street when George Phelps and LeeRoy Morgan came out of the bank shooting. Ray Matthews was waiting at the curb for them with a souped-up '49 Ford with the motor running . . . but hell, it was in all the papers. You can look it up for yourself.

Thirty Four

It's 1960 now, and the Springs is growing fast. Some of the city fathers are even predicting we'll get to half a million people by the end of the century. We'll see. But I do know for a fact that my caseload keeps getting bigger every year, and the crimes . . . the rapes, and murders, the mutilations, kidnappings and armed robberies . . . just keep coming. Which brings me back to the beginning, and the Whim-Wham man.

I think the Whim-Wham man was a victim, the same as my sister Catherine and Maddie . . . and I think the same monster killed all three of them . . . the man who called himself Petey.

It took me a long time to piece it all together, but Petey's the one who did it. There's no doubt in my mind, because Petey, like the Whim-Wham man, had the means and the opportunity: a knife and a place of concealment in which to do the deed. The difference is motive. I don't believe the Whim-Wham man had the capacity to rape, or the desire to kill. He liked little girls, no doubt about it, but he liked bunnies, and kittens, and puppies too. He saw them as things to admire and pet.

They were soft, and smelled good; they were pretty and playful, and weren't scared of him. I don't think he had thoughts of a sexual nature, any more than a five-year-old does. He just didn't have the capacity for it. Petey, however, was a whole different kettle o' fish, as Ma says. There was something twisted and bent in him. Tony confirmed that, when he told me why he fired him. And Petey did what he did to the Whim-Wham man with no more thought or emotion than if he were cleaning fish or cutting up a chicken for Sunday dinner. Then, after hacking the testicles off of a living, breathing human being in front of five witnesses, he strangled him to death, disposed of the evidence right in front of us, and sauntered away in the dark. It takes a monster to do something like that . . . and I think he'd done it before.

There's no word to describe someone like the man who called himself Petey, persons without a conscience, who commit depraved acts to fulfill some sick need of their own. I saw a few of them during the war . . . they cut off ears or tongues from enemy soldiers to put on shoelaces as reminders of the men they killed . . . those same monsters sometimes carried pliers in their pockets to pull the gold teeth from the mouths of the dead.

I know Petey did it because of the size of the knife wounds on Catherine and Maddie. The Whim-Wham man only had a pocket knife—and it was too small to have made the wounds I saw on their bodies. Those marks came from a bigger knife . . . like the one Petey always carried on his right hip . . . the same one he destroyed in the fire after he'd killed the Whim-Wham man.

The last aspect of my case against Petey is conjecture, pure and simple, but I think Petey, or whatever his name is, had done it before, and then after, he was here. In 1937 or early 1938, a little girl, ten years old, was raped and murdered in Fort Collins, Colorado, in the same way: stabbed more than forty times with a heavy knife, when she and her little brother got separated in the woods along the railroad tracks, looking for their lost dog Chipper.

I think it happened like this: After Tony threw him out, Petey migrated down to the hobo camp by the wood trestle bridge, in order to catch a train. It wasn't far from where the Whim-Wham man was camped. Something triggered him, getting fired and run off maybe, and he saw the two girls, either playing or picking flowers after they'd talked to the Whim-Wham man, and he'd given Catherine the cat carving. Petey overpowered and murdered both of them, one after the other. Then, when he heard the searchers, he joined right in. As more and more men piled in, who knew—in all of the confusion—that he wasn't a real searcher at all. Who could've even guessed the evildoer was right in our midst, or that in a master stroke of manipulation, he'd managed to convict and execute . . . with my help . . . an innocent man. It is a mortal sin I'll answer to God for someday. I burn with humiliation when I remember that soulless monster, riding in Mr. Brickman's pickup truck with me, advising me about the moral high road. He must have been chortling with glee at my naïveté.

In the meantime, with whatever time I have left on earth, I'm doing all I can to make what amends I can. I've taken no wife. How could I, with such a moral and legal affair hanging over me? If the priests are right, wouldn't my sins be passed along to any sons or daughters I might father? Isn't that what they mean by the concept of original sin?

I've dedicated my life to the eradication of monsters like Petey. When I first became a detective, I chased all over hell and half of Georgia trying to catch him, but I was always too late. By the time I heard about it, Petey, or whomever the killer was, had moved on. They're hard to find, harder to catch, and even hard to kill. But I do what I can and have had some modest successes from time-to-time. Maybe I'll put them into future journals. We'll have to wait and see.

I've kept files on unsolved murders of little girls in the south and western parts of the country, anywhere I think a monster like Petey will, or could roam. I accumulated a whole file drawer of them during the 1950s alone. It's how I'm sure Petey is a multiple murderer. In the past ten years, little girls were stabbed and murdered in New Mexico, Texas, Louisiana, Florida, Utah, Colorado, Arizona—and those are just the ones that got written about in the newspapers and sent to me by the clipping service I use. They cut out the articles and mail them to me. I feel like I'm only scratching the surface too. Who knows how many little kids, boys as well as girls, disappear and are never found? We don't keep statistics on that information at the city level, let alone the county, state or federal level. So far, I'm a one-man band. Law enforcement types are hard to convince that monsters are out there, or that their crimes are repeated, over and over again; it's much easier after all, to believe that our police and courts and jails are infallible; it makes me wonder, how many innocent men are incarcerated or executed . . . and how many monsters like Petey are running around out here in the real world, passing us on the street . . . or living right next door? I hope it will get better in the future. They say we'll have machines then that won't forget anything—computers like the ones that launch all the satellites we've got now, in outer space. I'm not holding my breath though.

The Whim-Wham man still comes to me in my dreams, when I relive the terrible day and night that's delineated my life since then. After Petey's done the deed and burned the evidence, and disappeared . . . the Whim-Wham man's eyes open in my dream, and stare at me. He doesn't, can't speak, but his eyes are always looking into mine and always seem to say, *Why? How? What?* without words, and I wake, bathed in cold sweat, tangled in the sheets, unable to go back to sleep that night.

Whenever I go up to see Ma and Annie in Palmer Lake, I stop, hike down to where the Whim-Wham man is buried and tell him once again how sorry I am. I let him know too, the latest news about my hunt for the monster who called himself Petey. Then, surrounded by the illusions and ghosts of the past, I leave him, go back to continue the hunt. I'll never stop until I find Petey and dispense the .45-caliber justice I promised Catherine I would, all those years ago.

I still have the carving of the manx cat. It's shiny now and worn smooth by my fingers over the years, still stained with Catherine's blood. Its simple form and lifelike appearance never fail to charm me and serve as a reminder that talent and beauty and grace are found in the unlikeliest places and hands . . . if only we're smart enough to see and appreciate it . . . no matter what form it appears in. And last, I hope that wherever he is, the Whim-Wham man has fair weather and easy living, that it's always summertime and the animals come out with the morning sun to run and leap and play for him while he whittles and carves them in wood . . . that he always finds a sharp knife close at hand . . . and sleeps peacefully through each and every night in a heaven where monsters never tread.

ACKNOWLEDGEMENTS

Book projects begin with a solitary effort by a lone individual, but in the end, they become collaborations in order to be successfully finished and put into your hands. I would like to publicly thank each of the following individuals and organizations for their invaluable help:

The Pioneers Museum of Colorado Springs, archivist Laura Fuller, The Starsmore Center for Local History and a special thank you for his friendship and generosity to Historical Western America Art Collector and Philanthropist, Nelson A. "Buz" Rieger, without whom the George Caleb Bigham masterpiece, *Mountain Landscape 1878*, would neither be hanging in the Pioneers' Museum, nor gracing the cover of this book. Additional information about the painting and Mr. Rieger is in a following section entitled: *About the Cover*;

Donald R. Kallaus, for his meticulous work and attention to the infinite number of tiny, unnoticed details that go into the design, lettering and formatting of both the interior and exterior of the book you're holding in your hands; all of our friends at Lightning Source and Ingram; Allison Auch, for her precise and careful editing and for making me look smarter than I am; Lora Brown, for her dedicated hard work, can-do, will-do, it's done attitude, and without whom I'd be lost; Webmaster, Michael Kimbrell; Marketing and Web Strategist, Susan McKenna; eBook Formatter, Jonathan Scott; First Readers: Bob Will, Mike Curley, Mary Gene Lynn, Skip Mooney and Susan Rieger;

Technical Advisors: Dick Reisler, Steve Kautz, Joe Jiardine, and Bert Entwistle, who each kept me from errors of fact; My wife of thirty-six years, June McKenna, whose encouragement, loving care and kindness has enabled me to find my talent as a writer. And last . . . Thank You to each and every one of you, my loyal fans and readers everywhere, who've read and recommended my books to others.

—JDM

A Rhyolite Press Readers Guide To

_____

The Whim-Wham Man

_____

John Dwaine McKenna

Questions for Discussion

There is a distinct difference between bums, hobos, and tramps. Do you know what they are? Do you think it helps to define them, or do you think they're all just homeless military vets or drug and alcohol abusers? What do think should be done about them? Do you think they can or will change? Do you think the problem was bigger or smaller during the Great Depression than it is today?

In chapter 7 and again in chapter 9, Jamey McGoran describes his two meals at the Brickman's house in great detail. Why do you think this is? Do you think he was getting enough to eat at home? Did anyone notice that while "Tony was having specials on roast chicken" at the Hardy House because "Ma thinned out her hens and a couple of roosters," that there was no meat at the McGoran house other than some venison jerky? Discuss the implications of this.

Chapter 15 is a graphic depiction of extreme violence, cruelty and depravity. Discuss the effect you think it would have on yourself, if you were in Jamey's position at the age of fifteen.
Do you think he meant it when he vowed revenge? And, will he be able to carry it out?
What do you think will heal Jamey?

In chapter 16, as Mr. Brickman and Jamey are setting out to find Maddie, Mrs. Brickman whispers something to her husband. What do you think she said?

In chapter 20, one of the most poignant scenes in the book happens when both mothers are hugging and trying to comfort each other. How did you react to it?

Discuss your emotional responses. Is there a consensus?

I believe that we humans are insane when in a total drunken state; we'll say, do or act out anything that enters our altered mind. Mood swings can and do take place in an instant, and sometimes bring deadly consequences. In chapter 21 and 28 Jamey McGoran describes the mood changes as his father consumes more and more alcohol. Were the scenes and the descriptions accurate in your opinion?

In chapter 22, Eileen McGoran (Ma) gives Jamey the manx cat carving. Is she urging him to seek revenge? Discuss what you think is going on here?

In 23, when Petey tells Jamey "It's a hard hard road . . ." what do you think he was saying, and why? Does it imply that Petey has a conscience . . . or not? Is he counseling Jamey, or just feeling sorry for himself?

In chapter 32, in the recruiting office: "The Gunney spun his chair off to one side, looking out the window and thinking for a long while . . . "

What and why, was he reflecting about?

Why did Jamey, change his name to Jake McKern?

If you have other thoughts or comments or questions you'd like us to answer, email them to:

Lora@rhyolitepress.com

She answers them on Tuesday and Thursday afternoons in the order received.

A Conversation with John Dwaine McKenna

The interview took place in Colorado Springs in June 2012. The questioner is Ms. Betsy Cary of the LEW (League of Enlightened Women).

The Whim-Wham Man is an awfully intense story for such a compact book—a lot happens in just a few days—heartbreaking things. I'm wondering, what gave you the idea for it?

Back in January of 2011, when our then Governor, Bill Ritter was leaving office due to term limits, I noticed a small one column inch piece buried in the back pages of our local newspaper that said he'd issued a full pardon for a man named Joe Arridy, who'd been executed in 1939. Governor Ritter called the execution "a travesty." To me, that was like throwing a grilled pork chop to a hungry hound. I had to know more. It turned out that Arridy was a mentally-impaired man whose IQ was so deficient he was incapable of performing a routine task such as mopping the floor . . . he'd forget what he was doing and become confused and emotionally distraught. He was incapable of caring for himself and, in a just world, would have been institutionalized. He wasn't however, and when he was found wandering around in Cheyenne, Wyoming after hopping a freight train in Pueblo, Colorado with some other boys who abandoned him a few days later, the local sheriff coerced a confession from him in which Arridy admitted to the murders of two little girls in Pueblo. When the facts the Sheriff wrote didn't fit the crime, he said the victims were bludgeoned, which wasn't true, they were murdered with a hatchet, he rewrote the confession and had Arridy re-sign it. The reason? So that the sheriff could, and indeed did collect a $1,000 reward for apprehending the so-called perpetrator.

Meanwhile, back in Pueblo, another man named Frank Aguilar, a handyman for the murdered girls father, confessed to the crime and produced the actual murder weapon. He was executed in 1937, two full years before Arridy, whom he exonerated. But public opinion was against Joe Arridy and he had no defenders. His parents were impoverished immigrants who barely understood English, and couldn't help by hiring legal counsel, so in 1939 Arridy went to the gas chamber at 'Old Max' in Canon City. Thirty minutes before his scheduled execution he was playing with a toy train that he gave to another inmate saying, "You can have this. I gotta go get executed now." He was 24 years old. Legend has it that the warden wept.

So Arridy was The Whim-Wham Man?

He inspired him, yes. But the Whim-Wham Man took on a life and a character all his own as the story was written. He's more complex than he first appears.

How so? Did it take long to write the story?

It took nine months of focused and concentrated effort to write. I put a lot of thought into each character and some scenes were difficult to write because I always project myself into them and the characters too; at least in my mind. Some scenes brought me to tears, and still can, even though I've read it many, many, many times.

The other question was . . .

The complexity of The Whim-Wham Man?

Oh, Yeah. The Whim-Wham Man, like all the characters in the book, are more complex than they appear because of what they don't say, and therefore what they imply. For example, why had the Whim-Wham Man been traveling so long and so far? What's his history? Where does he come from? How and where did he learn to whittle or carve? Does he have roots somewhere? A family? Is he capable of appreciating his life? Is he happy doing what he's doing? He's living rough, like an animal, does he know anything else? Is he capable of living any other life? And the biggie: is the Whim-Wham Man's life worth living? Is he, as Sheriff Malone implies when he says, "One bum more or less don't mean shit to me," expendable? Is this how society, all of us, see people like the Whim-Wham Man? That their lives just aren't worth living . . . that they are invisible and expendable? The paradox of the Whim-Wham Man is that he exposes a lot of answers without asking questions. He makes all of us examine our hearts as his tragedy is overshadowed by the murder of two little girls.

What kind of answers? Could you be specific, give some examples?

Sure. Here's one: when the vigilantes first arrive on the scene and Petey attacks the Whim-Wham Man as he's sleeping, no one tries to talk to him, give him a chance to say anything; he has no defense whatsoever, either figuratively or literally. Everyone assumes he did it, that the Whim-Wham Man is the killer. No one notices or points out the fact that even though he hasn't bathed or changed his clothes in days or weeks, the Whim-Wham Man has no sign of blood on himself. We all, vigilantes and readers alike, accept his guilt as a given. It isn't until the denouement of the story, when Jake McKern is summing up the case, that we learn that the Whim-Wham Man was in fact innocent, as much a victim as Catherine and Maddie. His innocence is what fuels

McKerns guilt. It's why McKern, like Lady MacBeth, can never cleanse himself of guilt: the murder of an innocent.

Hmmm, that's heavy. I'll think about that for awhile ... What about other characters ... Jamey McGoran, for one, he seems pretty straightforward to me. Is he?

No, not actually. He's really two characters, Jamey McGoran and Jake McKern, and they're both driven by different emotions; Jamey's motivated by revenge, Jake McKern by guilt, but they're two different people as unique as snowflakes, but as mysterious and complex as the Antikythera mechanism ...

That's the ancient computer found off the coast of Greece, isn't it?

Yes. It's a device for calculating astronomical events. Maybe that was a bad comparison ...

Not at all. But we'd like to know more about Jamey, or Jake.

I'll go with Jake since that's who'll he'll be from now on. Jake McKern will be a serial character. We'll see more of him in the future, where he'll be a law and order man, but a conflicted one who's always trying to atone for his past. His guilt about the death of the Whim-Wham Man, and his anger about not ever finding Petey to avenge his sister and Maddies' murders eat at him. His conscience won't ever be still.

So we can expected more books from you featuring Jake McKern?

Yes. Absolutely.

Well I for one am looking forward to it. Thank-you for talking to us today.

You're welcome. I was honored to do so.

About the Author

John Dwaine McKenna is the author of the widely-acclaimed and award-winning book, *The Neversink Chronicles*, and his column, *The Mysterious Book Report* appears weekly in *The Tri-Valley Townsman*. He lives in southern Colorado with his wife June. See his blogs at **johndwainemckenna.com**

About The Painting

The cover of The Whim Wham Man continues a Rhyolite Press innovation that began with the publication of our award-winning *The Neversink Chronicles*: a historic painting as the focal point of the cover of certain books with a period essence.

The painting which graces the front of *The Whim-Wham Man* is a 28 by 44 inch masterpiece by American Artist George Caleb Bingham entitled simply *Mountain Landscape 1878*, and is the last large work done by Bingham before his death in 1879. It appears here by permission and license of The Colorado Springs Pioneers Museum Starsmore Center for Local History, 215 S. Tejon Street, Colorado Springs, CO 80903, where we were assisted by archivist Laura Fuller. George Caleb Bingham's *Mountain Landscape 1878* is believed by many of us to be a depiction of Pikes Peak as viewed from the Denver & Rio Grande RR tracks just southeast of the hamlet of Greenland, Colorado. Controversy exists however, as art experts have pointed out similarities to another painting of New Hampshire's Mt. Washington. A fascinating booklet about the discovery of the painting and the attribution thereof by Nelson A. "Buz" Rieger is available by contacting the Pioneers Museum where *Mountain Landscape 1878* by George Caleb Bingham resides, when not on tour or loan . . . having been donated by Mr. and Mrs. Rieger, who, as patrons, collectors and philanthropists, have done so much to preserve our western art heritage. We, the art-appreciating public, are indebted to the Riegers for their foresight, dedication, and yes, for their generosity. From one who literally got chills when I first saw Binghams 1878 masterpiece, a humble thank-you does not seem like nearly enough.

　　　　　　—JDM

About the Type

The *Whim-Wham Man* is set in Adobe Minion Pro.

Minion is an old style serif typeface inspired by letters used during the late Renaissance-era. It was designed in 1990 by Robert Slimbach for Adobe Systems. It has proven to be a popular and adaptive type, used for everything from Stieg Larsson's Millennium Trilogy to other languages including Arabic, Cyrillic, Hebrew, Thai, and Song (Chinese). Minion is noted for its versatility, warmth and balance, making it one of the most readable and widely-used fonts available today.

Have you seen
our other
Rhyolite Press
Publications . . .

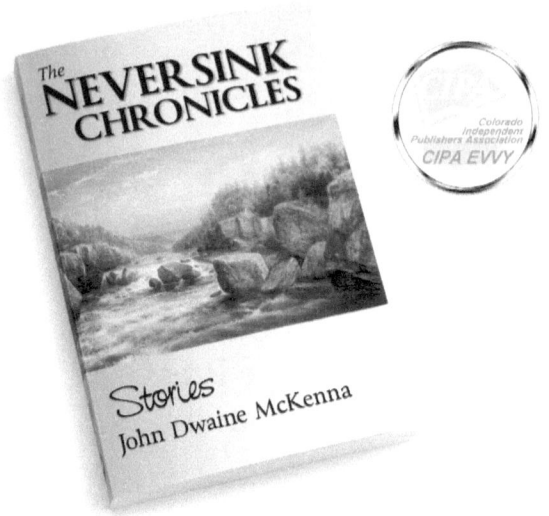

WHEN THE STAKES ARE THE AIR WE BREATHE,
THE WATER WE DRINK
AND THE LAND WE GROW OUR FOOD ON . . .
YOU'D BETTER HOPE JACK BANNISTER IS ON THE JOB!

THE DRIFT

An Environmental Thriller combined with a hundred year old
mystery and treasure hunt!
An intense cat-and-mouse game featuring Special Agent Jack
Bannister takes place deep in the mines beneath the mountains
of Cripple Creek, Colorado with life and death consequences.

Don't miss this exciting debut!

$15 at bookstores everywhere, or direct from the publisher:
www.rhyolitepress.com

ISBN 978-0-9839952-2-7
eBook: ISBN 978-0-9839952-5-8

Coming in Spring of 2013 . . .

THE COLORADO *Noir* CHRONICLES

"Stories from the other Colorado
Springs . . . the one the tourists aren't
allowed to see . . . where the marginal
ones live and die in
the shadows of affluence."

www.ingramcontent.com/pod-product-compliance
Lightning Source LLC
Chambersburg PA
CBHW020640250626
47154CB00008B/2764